THE EMPTY T

Lloyd sat wit
ning out of his
the gag. He co
chest and belly
never be the sa
not go back to ... efore. He had
learned, abrupt... special kind of hatred. He thought he could not hate any more violently than he did in those moments. The next hour tempered it, like a cherry red blade thrust into the quenching oil . . .

Also by John D. MacDonald
in Magnum Books

A KEY TO THE SUITE
DEAD LOW TIDE
SOFT TOUCH
LAST ONE LEFT
YOU LIVE ONCE
DEATH TRAP
THE ONLY GIRL IN THE GAME
THE EXECUTIONERS
THE DROWNER

JOHN D. MacDONALD

The Empty Trap

MAGNUM BOOKS
Methuen Paperbacks Ltd

A Magnum Book

THE EMPTY TRAP
ISBN 0 417 04540 9

First published in USA 1957
by Fawcett World Library
First published in Great Britain 1980
by Magnum Books

Magnum Books are published
by Methuen Paperbacks Ltd
11 New Fetter Lane, London EC4P 4EE

Made and printed in Great Britain
by Hazell Watson & Viney Ltd
Aylesbury, Bucks

THE EMPTY TRAP

1

The clouds were low over the mountains. The two cars had climbed the graveled road up out of the night into the first light of dawn. At times there would be a break in the cloud level and through them he could see the brown peaks above timberline touched with the gold and pink of the rising sun.

He was in the lead car, the dark blue Chrysler with Nevada plates. Tulsa Haynes drove slowly, big hands on the wheel. The world had been black shadows, with yellow headlights moving cautiously ahead. Now first light brought color into the world, a bronze to the backs of Tulsa's hands, a blue gleam to the car hood. Tulsa turned the lights off and, moments later, the lights of the Pontiac that followed closely went off and the two cars moved up the mountain curves of the grey road.

He was in the middle, between Tulsa and Valerez. He sat awkwardly, wrists bound behind him, ankles lashed together, both tied tightly with a sheer nylon stocking, gossamer thin, unbreakably strong. Valerez, at Tulsa's order, had unknotted the gag shortly after they had driven away from the Motel Montañas, had pulled the strip of toweling out of Lloyd's mouth and dropped it out the side window. It was cold up in the dawn mountains. He could smell the dried acid of the perspiration on his clothing, the sweat of pain and fear. And he could smell the stink of his burned chest.

Valerez had just lighted another cigarette. Back in the motel Lloyd had seen the name on the packet. Delicados. Valerez held the cigarette to Lloyd's lips. The paper had a sugary taste. The smoke was raw and strong when he sucked it down into his lungs.

Tulsa had been going more slowly, watching the drop at the right side of the road. He stopped. "You think it's okay, Giz?"

"It is wild country. But we should look, maybe."

Tulsa turned off the motor, took the key out, set the parking brake hard. Lloyd knew he took no chances. At no time had he left any opening. He was a professional. They got out and walked up ahead of the car, walked fifty feet. Benny, who had been driving the Pontiac, hurried to join them. There was no need for Benny to take precautions. Sylvia, his only passenger, was dead.

Lloyd Wescott watched them. They pointed over the drop. It was very still in the mountains, with no sound of bird or insect. They talked together and he could not hear them. Tulsa stood with his big hands on his hips. Had he not been beside the others, his breadth of shoulder would have made him look shorter than his six feet. He wore tailored khakis, skin-tight at the waist, taut around lean hips. The short stiff black hair was like a cap, and when the sun broke through, Lloyd saw a pink highlight on Tulsa's quarter profile, on the high hard cheekbone. Benny, the squat little man with the clown face, pranced and gesticulated as he talked. Valerez, the stranger, had put his dark suit coat on over the pink shirt, the dark maroon knit tie with the ruby pin. His black hair gleamed above the pale, narrow, handsome face, and he stood a little apart from the other two.

Careful selection of grave, Lloyd thought. And I can be grateful to them for one thing. There isn't any room in me for fear, or regret or remorse. No room for anything but hate. Life ends here. The lights go out. I should be thinking about eternity, and remembering, in this last time left to me, all the bright days of my life. And all I can think about is how I want to see them dead.

Tulsa made a gesture of impatience, of decision, then sent Benny back to the Pontiac. Tulsa returned to the Chrysler, leaned on the window frame on the driver's side and looked in at Lloyd.

"I'll make it easy," he said.

"Thanks." The word was blurred by Lloyd's broken mouth.

"You got more guts than I figured, boy. Harry said make it rough for both of you. She got it rough. But the way I figure, she knew what she was doing, and you got suckered along. This wasn't your league, Lloyd. So I'll make it easy. You won't know about it."

"Don't . . . do me any favors."

"I'll let Harry know you took it good. And she took it bad."

Benny swung the Pontiac around the Chrysler, brought it to a precise stop aimed at an angle toward the drop. Tulsa said to Valerez, "How soon before anybody finds them?"

"One cannot say. A week, a month, maybe one hour. But it does not matter."

"What the hell do you mean?"

"These people, you think they call the policia? There will be things of value, perhaps pieces of the car to be taken to a village, sold for a few centavos."

Tulsa snapped his thick fingers. "God damn. I nearly forgot. Harry woulda chewed me good. Benny!"

"Yeah?"

"Get those rings off her."

"Rings? Sure." He dived back into the Pontiac. After a few moments he called to Tulsa, "They're on tight."

"Those rings are worth three grand," Tulsa said. "Harry told me before he married her."

"Thirty-six thousand pesos," Valerez said wistfully.

Benny came back with the rings and gave them to Tulsa. Benny looked in brightly at Lloyd. "How they breaking, pal?"

"Cut his ankles loose, Giz," Tulsa said. Valerez leaned in and, with quick blade thrust, deftly slit the nylon at his ankles. Tulsa pulled him out the other side of the car and set him on his feet. Lloyd's knees sagged. Tulsa cursed and bent as though to carry him over his shoulder. Lloyd felt there might be one slim chance if he kept on his feet. Not a chance to save himself. It had gone far beyond that.

"Can walk," he said, and locked his knees. The pain of the burned feet was excruciating.

"A gutsy guy," Benny said admiringly. "He maybe was in the wrong business, Tuls."

They held his arms, Tulsa on his left, Benny on his right, and walked him toward the Pontiac. He walked as steadily and as strongly as he could, forcing himself with what was left of strength and will. Tulsa did not relax his hold, but Benny did. He felt the slackening of the grip. He timed his steps, summoned up the last bit of explosive energy in deadened muscles, then lunged hard to his right. Tulsa hauled him back. But his shoulder had slammed hard into Benny's. Benny lost his grip and staggered toward the brink, giving a shrill yelp of fright. He fell, scrabbling at the gravel, half over, sliding further, yelling again. Valerez reached him at the last instant, caught his wrist. They were both poised there and Lloyd tried to dive at them, to take both of them over with him, but Tulsa held him. All energy gone, Lloyd sagged to his knees. Valerez pulled Benny back onto the road. Benny sat, his face grey, cursing thickly. He got up slowly, came over and kicked Lloyd in the side.

"God damn, Tuls," he said. "I'm shakin' all over. Jesus!" He kicked Lloyd again, heavily.

"Cut it out," Tulsa said. "Get him on his feet."

"I've always been scared of falling off something high."

When they stood him up, Lloyd thought he wouldn't be able to speak, but he managed to say, "Then . . . that's the . . . way you're . . . going to die . . . Benny."

"What the hell do you mean?"

"Everybody . . . dies the way . . . they're scared of."

"Hey, is he kiddin' me, Tuls? Is he?"

"Shut up. Get the door open there."

Tulsa put him in the car, behind the wheel. Sylvia was slumped against the door on the far side, body slack in death, black hair wreathing the side of the empurpled face. Benny had dressed her after death, dressed her in the yellow short-sleeved sweater, the pistachio flannel skirt. Tulsa gave an order, and Valerez and Benny Bernholz went over the car, wiping it clean.

"When I say go, push with your shoulders," he said. "Don't touch it."

Tulsa reached a heavy arm through the window, a spring-handled sap in his hand. "This'll make it easier," he said. He snapped the lead end of the sap against Lloyd's forehead with a backhanded twist of his wrist. Lloyd moved instinctively, and just quickly enough so that it glanced off the side of his forehead, just ahead of the temple. One of the familiar pain-flowers bloomed and burst in gaudy blue and white and at the other end of an echoing tunnel he heard Tulsa yell, "Push!"

He could not move, but he could see straight ahead. "Wait," Tulsa yelled and he held the car back with his great strength. Lloyd was only partially aware when Valerez reached in, cut the nylon from his wrists. Again they pushed. The car moved forward. The right front corner dropped first. It happened so very slowly. Now, he thought, that thing they talk about is happening!

I argued with the salesman about this car, about his offer. The red and white hardtop convertible. He wanted fourteen hundred difference and I wanted to trade for a thousand. When I went into the sales manager's office, the air conditioning was turned very low. There was an award certificate on the wall. We could not get anywhere until I told him I was the manager at the Hotel Green Oasis, and then the atmosphere was more cordial and we traded for eleven fifty and I drove it back, and it smelled new and it ran well, and that was the week Harry Danton brought Sylvia back from Los Angeles and they moved into the hotel.

It dropped on the right side, and he was thrown against Sylvia's body and for one moment he could look down the long cruel slant of steep brown rock, at small wiry trees that grew out of the rock, and then the roll and fall continued a clanging and crashing and a steep sickness, and then he spun high and free and he saw the car and the mountains turn around him and knew he was apart from the car. Then, in the turn, the brown rocks came up to a smash of whiteness against his face, a floodlight whiteness that dwindled down and away like the last white spot on a cooling TV picture tube.

He knew he was cold. There were great sounds around him. It was very difficult to think. Needles of cold beat against his face. He turned his face slowly and with great difficulty until his cheek touched a sharp edge. He opened his eyes and he saw wet rock inches from his eyes. The rain drove against wet rock, exploding into silvery mist. There was a blue glare of lightning and then thunder cracked loudly and the long echoes boomed and rolled through the mountains. Slowly he began to know that he was bent oddly, body arched back at the waist, something hard across the small of his back. Lightning was close for a long time, and then moved away and the rain slackened and stopped. He felt rigid with cold. Almost at once the sun came out, a high white glare over the mountains, and the wet rocks began to steam. He could not think why he was here, where this place was, why he should be made so uncomfortable. When he tried to move pain brought a threatening blackness. His right hand and arm seemed willing to move when he willed it. He brought his right hand up close to his face. He turned his hand over and looked with distant curiosity, with a clinical remoteness, at the great tear in the heel of his palm, at the thick flap of skin and flesh that lay back over his wrist. It bled slowly.

Inch by painful inch he turned his body to the right, toward the cliff face, moving his face back from the corner of rock. The hardness that had been across his back now bit into his waist. After another few inches he turned the rest of the way suddenly and the hard thing was across his belly and he was jackknifed across it. And he looked down a steep sickening slant. There was brown rock and sun on steaming brown rock, and a few trees with knotted trunks no bigger than his forearm. Far below him he saw a patch of color, of red and white. He closed his eyes. The height made him feel sick. When he could look again, he knew it was the car. His car. His mind and memory until that moment had been like a dry stream bed. The single act of recognition of the car was like opening a dam at the head of the stream. The waters came roaring down, turbulent, filling it from brim to brim.

He closed his eyes again. Blood pounded in his head. Have to think, he told himself. Hanging across a tree. Broken all to hell. Thrown clear. Ought to be dead. Can very easily become dead. Just wiggle a little. Slide off the tree. Never feel a thing after the first bounce.

But it would be nice to see Tulsa Haynes. And Benny Bernholz. And Giz Valerez. And Harry Danton. Maybe, most of all, Harry Danton.

He felt as though the tree was slowly cutting him in half. He could see his legs, ankles, feet. Both shoes were gone. His left foot was twisted crazily to the side, the ankle big as a melon. Blood dripped from the toes of the right foot. He tried to swallow and could not. His entire face felt numb below the eyes. He touched his face with the fingers of his right hand. He could not identify what he felt. Bone in the wrong place. Splintered things that could be teeth. He let the right arm hang. He wept for himself, wept for the broken body. This was the gateway to death; he was a half step away.

He felt unconsciousness coming, the way a night shadow moves across a lawn. He fought it back. He looked down again. There was the steep drop. Close below the tree was a ledge. It was more of a crevasse than a ledge. The ledge tilted back. He did not see how he could lower himself to it, lower himself gently enough to keep from continuing on down the slope. But life or death had narrowed down to this one lean chance, with the probability that even if he could manage it, death would only be delayed. He knew he was close to passing out. He caught the trunk of the tree in his torn right hand, and using the leverage, he began to worm his way back. The trunk was across his diaphragm, then his chest. He hooked his left elbow over it, moved further. When the trunk came under his chin, the almost useless left arm slipped. The trunk hit him under the chin. His feet swung against the rock and he made a thin squeaking sound when his left ankle banged. His right hand began to slip as his weight slowly opened his fingers. But as his hand opened the toes of his right foot touched the ledge. He found precarious balance, and when he let go with his hand, he fell against the cliff face, supported by his right foot. He caught an edge of rock with his right hand as he started to topple. It delayed him slightly, but then he fell full on his back, head snapping back to strike the rock, and the shadow moved quickly over him, the world turning dark.

When he came to, it was a world of blue-gray. He could see the sun on the high peaks across the valley. It took him several moments to decide that it must be nearly night rather than dawn. He watched the sun line move up the peaks. He was thirsty and his body had stiffened. He moved gingerly, painfully, trying to make himself more comfortable. If this was the place to wait for death on this night, then be comfortable, if you can. When the blackness came again, it was not like sleep.

He awoke and stars were high and he felt he was on fire. In the night he babbled and yelled and had strange bright visions. The yells echoed faintly from the far mountain wall of the deep valley. At dawn the visions were gone and he was cold. In the morning there was rain, another heavy rain. He held his face in the rain, and though he did not have enough feeling in his face to know if his mouth was opened or closed, he felt the coolness trickle into his throat and he was able to swallow after a fashion. He pulled his shirt up with his right hand and squeezed the rain moisture from it into his mouth. The water brought him back from the dulled wait for death.

When he was able to look around, he saw that his ledge went narrowly around a shoulder of the cliff, and slanted down slightly. He worked himself over onto his belly. He could use his left elbow, his right hand and arm, his right leg. The left leg dangled. He inched himself along. He did not know how long it took to reach the shoulder of the cliff, one hour or six. There he could see the rest of the ledge. It opened out, almost as wide as a road, and went down steeply. After two hundred yards it reached a place where the mountain side was a different texture. There was a long sand slide, studded with round rocks and boulders. He followed it down with his eyes and saw that it ended at the valley floor where tropic growth was more luxuriant, where a rain-fed stream wound between the great stones that had tumbled down the flanks of the mountains.

The sun baked him, drying the moisture out of him. From the height of the sun he guessed it was early afternoon when he reached the long sand slide. He looked down at the water far below and knew he had to reach it. He looked back the way he had come and he felt pride. He laughed aloud and it was a curious croaking sound. He tried to say Harry Danton's name, but he could not articulate. He sensed the bright edge of delirium again, and fought back to logic and precarious sanity.

If he got onto the sand, he would go down. That was evident. But he could not go feet first. The left leg would crumple under him and turn him and he might roll. If that started, he would roll and bound among the hard stones. There had to be stability in the slide. The left arm had only limited usefulness. He would have to be able to see, and he would need some slightly effective method of steering himself. He thought about it a long time. Finally, with great effort, he tore a strip from his shirt. He crossed his ankles, left ankle across the right, and bound them clumsily. That way the left would not flop loose and dig into the sand. He eased himself out onto the sand slope. He moved slowly at first, head raised, elbows digging in. As he picked up speed he began to move directly toward a large boulder. The top inches of sand slid along with him. He dug the right elbow deeper and it swung him to the right. He almost lost control. He passed the rock so closely it gave his left elbow a sharp painful crack. This was the steering method the bobsledders used. He went faster. He was taking more sand along. The sand flowed over the smaller stones. He yelled in crazy triumph. Then there were more rocks ahead, and these were jagged ones. It was harder to steer. He clawed with his right hand, trying to dig himself sideways. He missed the rocks but he had lost stability. He had turned and began to roll. He rolled violently down the last of the slope, across hard ground, finally came to rest in the heart of a clump of dense shrubbery, unconscious.

In the blue of dusk, in the odd reflected light of the last of the sun on the mountains to the east, he crawled to the brook. He drank until his belly felt tight. He spewed up the water weakly and waited a long time and then drank sparingly. When he knew he would retain it, he crawled into the brush that would protect him from the morning sun.

2

In mid-morning he crawled out and drank. He had expected to feel stronger, but he felt weaker. He rolled onto his back, shaded his eyes, and looked up the dizzy cliff face. He tried to pick out his ledge, but he could not.

I got down from there, he thought. I got down alive. And it would have been a good trick for a whole man. I can tell myself I did that much. I have water and shade. Two ingredients. I need a doctor and food. What is today? It was the ninth of May when they found us. I went over the edge at dawn on the tenth. Yesterday was the eleventh. This will be the twelfth. Sunday morning then. A Sunday in May.

He tried to guess where he was in relation to the smashed car. He closed his eyes and tried to reconstruct how it had looked from the tree. At least it had not burned. It would be wise to get near the car, but not too far from the water. A man on a mountain might spot the car. He might climb down to investigate. There was that frail chance.

It should be in that direction, on the far side of the stream. Two hundred yards, perhaps. Maybe more. I can try it. There's nothing else to do.

He thought for a moment and then his heart began to pound. The car had not burned. Sylvia had liked to keep things in the glove compartment. Cookies, crackers, candy. Her appetite had never softened the trim lines of her body. There would be something there. Enough to give him another day, perhaps. Or two. He began the laborious crawl. He knew it was the only way he could move. Even if he could find a stick and pull himself erect, the bad leg and bad arm were on the same side. If only it could have been the right leg that was bad . . .

From time to time he strained up to see the terrain ahead. When the far bank looked better, he pulled himself through a shallow place in the stream, and took time out to soak himself in a pool a foot and a half deep. Water stung the hurts of his body, the knee and elbows raw with crawling.

On the far bank he found a bush with dark berries. He plucked several and could not decide how he could eat them. His jaw hung slack, badly broken, he knew. He pulped the berries in his fingers, and stuck them into the back of his throat, worked them down with his tongue. They were violently bitter and he coughed them out. The cookies and crackers would be a problem. Perhaps they could be pulped in water, in some sort of container, possibly a hub cap, and drunk like soup.

He moved on under the height of the sun. He stopped when he heard a curious sound, a flapping and croaking sound. He moved toward it. He saw a black ugly bird rise, croaking, tilt creaking wings and soar down again. Another bird came up and went down. He crawled and parted the brush and saw them in an open space, tearing, quarrelling, wings outspread, a tumult of hunger. He closed his eyes when a shift of the wind brought him the sour-sweet smell of what they had been fighting over. When he opened them again he saw, under the moving blackness, the soiled shreds of pistachio green and of yellow. He cawed at them, a furious sound of anger coming from the broken mouth at this ultimate indignity. He hurled small stones and crawled with painful haste. They went away and sat like deacons on the limbs of low barren trees, observing him. He could not look at what was left of Sylvia, could not bring himself to look. They seemed to recognize his weakness, and they moved closer.

For the rest of the afternoon, he worked with the furious energy of insanity. He used the stones close to her first, straining with the heavy ones. But there were not enough. He had to go further away each time, and many times he had to go so far they returned to her, the bolder ones, and he had to drive them away when he came back, pushing the stone along in front of him. He worked through the heat of the day with the mindless determination of a half crippled ant, and he made the cairn bigger and stronger than it had to be made.

Once it was done, his strength ebbed away from him and he lay on his back. The birds seemed to give up; some of them flew away. He watched them work themselves up out of the canyon, laboring up on black wings, circling higher until at last they came into the wind currents off the peaks and circled up there on motionless wings, in evil grace, before gliding off to some unknown place. But there were other birds who waited.

He turned his head and looked at the cairn. He wished he could speak aloud. But he could make the words in his head, and make them so clear he could read them as though he printed them carefully.

"This is a prayer. I have not prayed in many years. It isn't for me. It's for her. Her name was Sylvia. She sinned. She was a beautiful woman. She was twenty-six years old when she died. She died in terror and in shame and in degradation. She paid more than enough during the last hours she had on earth. She had her hell then. She doesn't need any more. Take care of her, somehow. Please."

He crawled to the stream and drank. He knew he could not crawl much farther. He knew the car would have to wait until the next day, if there would be a next day for him. He crawled into the shelter of the brush and lay on his back and watched, through green leaves, the end of the day. And he thought of how she had been in Mexico City.

They had driven down from Juarez in three days. The increasing distance had not given her peace of mind. Rather she had seemed to grow more frightened, day by day, pale, nervous, irritable.

"We're safe now," he told her.

"We'll never be safe. We shouldn't have done it. We shouldn't have tried to do it, Lloyd. We were crazy to try it. We were insane to even think of it. You don't know what they're capable of. You don't know how he'll feel about this. He can't let a thing like this go. We'll never be safe."

"Don't worry about it. Let me take care of things."

"You can't take care of things. You don't understand them. You don't know how they are."

She refused to be calmed. He found a small and inconspicuous hotel in Mexico City, a hotel with a parking lot in the rear where the car would be well concealed. He left the money locked in the trunk compartment. It seemed to be the safest place. He took ten of the hundred dollar bills. He had an idea how such things were managed. She refused to leave the small suite. He went out alone. He knew how careful he had to be. When they had been making plans he had managed to find out, without arousing suspicion, the names of those Latin American countries where citizenship could be arranged. There were three of them. He had no luck with the first consular official. His hints were coldly ignored. At the second place he had luck, even though the man made him uneasy.

The man was named Señor Rillardo, and he had a small unclean office, a look of greed, a rumpled suit, and very small fat white hands.

"You would like to become a citizen of my country?"

"Yes sir."

"It is necessary first to have a visa and then, after you are there, you make application for an immigrante permit.

Then, in two years, if there is approval, after simple tests, you receive first papers. You have a passport?"

"No sir."

"Ah! That makes a problem. What do you have?"

"This. My tourista card."

Rillardo took it and looked at it. "This is your name?"

"Yes, it is."

"You could get a passport, Meester Wescott?"

"I would not care to go back and ask for one. For personal reasons."

"For, perhaps, legal reasons?"

"I am not wanted by the law, Señor Rillardo."

Rillardo spread his small hands and said, "Then?"

"I have an enemy. A very powerful man."

"I see."

"I have understood that . . . in cases of emergency . . . your government is sometimes understanding. Certain shortcuts can be arranged."

Rillardo's face lost all expression. "It is possible. But such things can be very expensive."

"There is some money."

"How much?"

Lloyd smiled. "Isn't that the question I should be asking? Assume there is enough. What can you provide?"

"This is not a promise. I do not commit myself or my . . . associates, Meester Wescott. But if there was enough, this thing could be done. By personal examination and approval I could make of you a citizen of our nation, and I could issue you a passport here. Then air transportation could be most easily arranged. However, this is no guarantee against extradition. We do not offend our very powerful neighbor."

"No one will want to extradite me."

"I can name a figure. You must understand that I must make gifts to very many people. Our small country has a great number of officials. Many of them are men of great probity. For them the gifts must be ample. I would say, for you, it could be done for . . . in American dollars . . . twenty thousand."

"That is too much!"

Rillardo smiled sadly. "Safety is always expensive. Security is a rare commodity in a troubled world, my friend."

Lloyd thought for a moment. "Perhaps, if I were to make you a personal gift, Señor, completely aside from our transaction, it might be that you could talk your friends into a lower figure."

"A gift?"

Lloyd took out the automobile permit issued him when he had crossed the border and handed it to Rillardo. Rillardo pursed his lips. "Such things are difficult. There are Mexican customs to consider. It is not easy."

"Certainly you have friends in the Mexican customs department."

"Acquaintances, only. What is the color of this vehicle?"

"Red and white. A red like the border of that magazine on your desk. As you can see it's a recent model. It has fifteen thousand miles on it. It is a handsome car. I will have no further use for it . . . if we should have a meeting of the minds."

Rillardo laid the permit on his desk. "And what do you think would be a fair figure, Meester Wescott, for what you wish me to do for you?"

"May I first ask a question? If one lives quietly in your country, how much does it cost to live there, in American dollars?"

"Quietly? I must have more information."

"A small rented house not too far from a city. A full time maid and gardener. Good food. Perhaps a small swimming pool. Very little entertaining. Reasonably modern utilities."

"For that . . . for a man alone, I should say it could be done adequately, even with a certain style, for twenty-five hundred dollars a year."

Lloyd did a rapid computation. Say three thousand a year for two. Twenty from a hundred and ten would leave ninety. Thirty years.

"This is my offer, Señor Rillardo. I will pay the twenty thousand you ask. In cash."

The black eyebrows went up. "I do not understand?"

"For both of us. There are two of us. Here is her tourista card."

Rillardo took it and read the name aloud. "Miss Sylvia Kennedy. This is difficult. You make it difficult for me. Can you not be husband and wife?"

"Not legally. You can call us that, if you wish."

"I see. She was the woman of the man you speak of?"

"His wife. She used her birth certificate to get her card. She walked across the bridge."

"Perhaps you took the money of this man too?"

"That should not concern you, Señor."

"You are correct. I must apologize."

"Can it be done?"

Rillardo thought for a long time, frowning, fingering the corner of the auto permit. He smiled. "I can do it. But she must be called your wife."

"All right. What's the next step?"

"I must have ten thousand American dollars. I can issue the passport in two weeks time. There are certain things that must be checked first."

"Can you give me a receipt?"

"Of course not! That is absurd!"

"I will give you five thousand. I will give you the final amount when we board the plane."

"You make it more difficult."

"I am sorry."

Rillardo sighed heavily. "Then I shall arrange it your way. Have you the money here?"

"I will bring it to you."

"Today, please."

He took the five thousand back to Rillardo. The man counted it carefully, licking his white thumb. He folded it casually and put it in his inside jacket pocket.

"Two weeks from this day," he said. "That will be the seventeenth of May. A Friday. Reservations will be arranged for you and I will have the tickets here."

After he was standing again, Lloyd said, "We do not want to stay here in the city. We may be taking a chance to stay here. Can you suggest where we could go?"

Rillardo suggested they drive north on the Inter-American Highway to Zimapan and there turn west on the new road into the mountainous province of Queretaro. He was certain they could find a quiet place to stay.

On the way back to the hotel Lloyd felt entirely unreal. He felt as though he were taking a part in a half-forgotten movie. This was certainly not what his life had prepared him for—flight into a foreign land with another man's wife and money, dickering in a shabby office for illegal passports. He and Sylvia were to appear with pictures to be pasted on those purchased documents, sealed with the great seal of the nation of exile.

He was not so naive as to think it could go off without a hitch. There was the possibility that Rillardo would find the task too difficult. Then he would deny ever having seen Lloyd or having taken the five thousand. And there would be no way to prove it.

Or, it might be a private plane, and after the balance of the money had been taken from them, they might be dropped into the sea. Rillardo knew Lloyd had money, and knew Lloyd could not turn to his own government for help. Many risks could be taken to acquire the money of a helpless man. And Rillardo had an unsavory look about him.

Yet Lloyd was determined to make Sylvia feel that it was working out perfectly. That evening she had made him tell her over and over again how it would be for them, how they would be safe. She clung to him as though he was her last chance in all the world.

That night they left the city after dark and stayed in a hotel cottage in Zimapan. He had purchased Scotch. Sylvia drank until she was incoherent, until she passed out. He had never seen her drink so heavily. He was more than a little drunk himself. Her fear was infectious. He stood over the bed and looked down at the spill of dark hair, heard her thick breathing. This was not like the magic in the beginning. This had become furtive and sordid. He even thought of leaving her with half the money and driving hard for the border, crossing at, say, Matamoros into Brownsville, and trying to lose himself in the states. But he knew he could never leave her. It was a curious twisted love, but it was strong, and he could not leave her.

He sat and brooded for a long time. He became very depressed. He was certain that, somehow, they were going to be robbed and left penniless in Mexico. Rillardo would arrange it somehow. He was a fool to carry it all around in one chunk. It should be spread out. That would provide a reserve. He gave it intent alcoholic consideration. He remembered the jar in the car, a wide-mouthed glass jar with a screw lid. It contained what was left of the peanut brittle Sylvia had bought at the gas station in Las Cruces. The car was beside the cottage. He got the jar and dumped the candy out. He took the money from the trunk compartment into the cottage. It was in a blue canvas gym bag. He had owned the zipper bag for a long time. Once upon a time he had used it to carry basketball gear in.

By wadding the bigger bills tightly, he was able to get forty thousand into the jar. That left about sixty-five in cash. If everything worked out, he would be able to come back one day and get the forty thousand. And if it didn't work out at all, the forty thousand would be a reserve for them. He felt very clever. He wanted to wake Sylvia up and explain to her how cleverly he was handling everything. He had thought of burying it in the ground. He looked around the cottage. The walls were paneled. He went out and got the tire iron. He chose a spot where the bathroom door opened against a wall of the bedroom. There were no light outlets there. He carefully pried off the quarter round, then pried one panel board loose at the floor level and pulled it back, yet not so far back it would pull the top molding free. The jar sat neatly on one of the cross joists, and seeing that it was exactly the right size made him feel his plan was more valid. He nailed the board and the molding back, using a towel to keep from marring the wood. The cottages were quite new. There was no reason why it should be disturbed for years. He put everything away and went to bed.

He did not remember hiding the money until he was thirty miles west of Zimapan, on the new road. Sylvia was surly and sullen with the pangs of hangover. When he told her about it, she reacted violently and they had a bitter quarrel, the worst quarrel yet. Finally he got her to admit the wisdom of what he had done.

The new road dipped close to the village of Talascatan and then climbed gently up the heart of a valley for a mile and a half, to the Montañas Motel, a new place on a hill overlooking the highway. It was secluded. Cars beside the units could not be seen from the road. The units were set very far apart. The sign said in Spanish and English that there were cooking facilities.

They stopped and the quarrel was forgotten. Their unit was at the end the farthest from the others. The owners were Swiss, a gentle couple who had lived in Mexico for many years, and who had managed a hotel at Acapulco until it was torn down to make room for a more flamboyant structure. They had saved their money, had speculated in oceanfront land, and had made enough to build this motel. They said business was slow because the road was new. Next year the new road would join the secondary road that ran from Rio Verde to San Luis Potosi, and there would then be a great deal of through traffic.

Lloyd registered as Mr. and Mrs. Wesley Floyd. Their unit was clean and new. There were two large double beds in the bedroom, a cot in the small living room. That night, in the barranca behind the motel, the insects made a night-long shrilling. She lay in his arms and whispered, "I think it's going to be all right, Lloyd darling. Tonight for the first time, I think we will . . . . be safe."

During the days they toasted in the sun behind the motel. In the evenings they walked down to Talascatan and sat at one of the tables in front of a small restaurant and cantina facing the square and watched the young people walk around and around the square with the stained fountain and grubby bandstand. They drank the dark strong beer called Dos Equis, and they ate great bowls of rich caldo gallego, and later walked hand in hand through the night, walked back to the Montañas Motel, slightly drunk on the beer, hand in hand and singing softly in the night. On those few nights it seemed to him that what they had done was both good and necessary. A marriage to Harry Danton could not be called a marriage. This woman was his now, and would be forever his.

They walked back on the night of the ninth and the stars were very clear and high. They walked by all the other units to their own place where there was a starlight gleam on the bumper of the Pontiac parked behind it, under their bedroom windows.

He unlocked the door and she went in first and the lights went on. Sylvia screamed once. Perhaps she screamed again, but by that time the portable radio was on at full volume. Lloyd had tried to fight Tulsa with his fists. Tulsa, grinning and clowning, had worked him back into a corner, wedged him there, big shoulder under Lloyd's chin holding him upright, while he ripped his big hands into Lloyd's middle, working him the way a fighter in training works the heavy bag. He worked him until Lloyd's arms flapped loose as empty sleeves, until his chin bounced idiotically on Tulsa's shoulder, teeth clicking, room bouncing in his dazed vision. Then Tulsa backed off, held his left palm flat against Lloyd's chest, chopped him three times in the face with an overhand right. With the last blow the room bulged, turned red, and collapsed around him like a tent.

When he came to, he was in a cane arm chair, hands tied together behind the chair, mouth wedged full of cloth. The door was ajar and he could hear voices out there, hear the Swiss talking to a stranger in Spanish. His chair was shoved over into a corner. Tulsa stood listening. Benny stood behind Sylvia, holding her close to him with one thick arm around her slim waist, a grimy hand flat across her mouth. Sylvia's black hair was tangled, her eyes wide and hot and furious.

The voices stopped and Valerez came into the room and shut the door. "He go now," Valerez said in clumsy English.

"What did he want?" Tulsa asked.

"Too many peoples he said for one place so it is more. I give him eight pesos."

Tulsa shrugged. He went to each of the three windows, checked to make certain the blinds were completely closed. He paused in front of Lloyd, lifted his chin up, looked down at him. "Good morning, baby! Had a nice little vacation? Had a nice honeymoon? Wait a minute! Hell, she's still married to Harry, so what do you call it? Couldn't be a honeymoon, now could it? You're a bright one, baby. If you wanted action, you should have done something not so risky. Like maybe jumping off the hotel roof."

Sylvia began to kick and writhe. Benny cursed her. Tulsa said, "Quiet the bitch down, Benny."

Benny spun her violently, hit her with one quick clean motion, and the noise of the blow was small and brutal. He caught her as she fell forward and grinned at Tulsa, evil and meaningful grin on the clown face. "Where at you want her, Tuls?"

"In the bedroom. Then we hunt the money."

They found it easily. Tulsa brought it in, pulled the table over under a light, dumped it out. Benny sat down and counted it with the professional skill of a bank teller, jotting down totals for each stack, packing the stacks neatly in the zipper bag. He totaled his figures and said, "Sixty-four thousand eight hundred and ten, Tulsa. It's supposed to be more than that, isn't it?"

"Harry couldn't tell for sure. You know how it is. They'd claim more anyhow, wouldn't they? Giz, keep an eye on the dish."

"Dish?" Valerez said, looking around helplessly.

"Watch the girl, stupid! And just watch her, nothing else."

Then they turned the radio up again. Tulsa took off his shirt. They took the gag out of Lloyd's mouth. He had felt pain before. Not this kind of pain. This was a white light that kept exploding in his head. When he bucked in the chair and tried to scream, Benny would clap the towel over his mouth. Lloyd knew he fainted, but he did not know how many times. He would have told a dozen times had the pain been smaller. But the pain came in bursts that prevented his speaking. And when the pain faded, a dull stubborn anger closed his mouth. "That's all there was," he would bellow. He shouted it a dozen times.

Tulsa finally straightened up, dropped the cigar, turned his foot on it. "I'll buy it, Benny. Stuff his mouth again. And go get that tequila."

"Aren't we going soon?"

Tulsa looked at his watch. Benny tied the gag roughly in place. Tulsa said, "We kill time. Valerez says we can find a good place not too far, but not in the dark. So we leave about four. It's after ten now."

Lloyd sat with his chin on his chest, the tears running out of his eyes, breathing hard, sobbing against the gag. He could smell the rich stink of his burned chest and belly, his burned feet. He knew he could never be the same person again. He knew he could not go back to what he had been before. He had learned, abruptly, a special kind of hatred. He thought he could not hate any more violently than he did in those moments. Yet an hour later the hatred was stronger. The next hour tempered it, like a cherry red blade thrust into the quenching oil.

"She wants come out!" Valerez called in a nervous tone.

"So let her come," Tulsa said.

Sylvia appeared in the doorway. Her jaw was bruised. But she stood proudly, her head up, her eyes furious. She looked beyond Tulsa and Benny at Lloyd and her face changed. She tried to come to him, and Benny thrust her back roughly. "Lloyd, darling!" she said. "What did you two do to him?"

Benny burlesqued shyness, rubbing the side of his foot on the floor. "Well, we had a sort of like a cook out."

"You filthy monsters," she said, and her eyes filled with tears. She looked at Tulsa. "Are you taking me back to Harry?"

"Harry don't want to have to look at you, Mrs. Danton. Harry all of a sudden got tired of you, like."

Lloyd saw her bite her lip, glance toward the blue

bag. "You've got the money. Why don't you go and leave us alone now. You've done enough to Lloyd."

Tulsa spoke patiently to her, an explanatory tone. "Harry wouldn't much like that. He said you should have a real hard time. Most of all you, Mrs. Danton. A worse time than Lloyd darling here on account of he didn't know the score as good as you know it."

She looked at him with spirit and with bravery. "All right, Tulsa. Beat me up. Or should Benny hold me?"

She wore the pale blue linen dress he had bought her in Mexico City, at the shop on Juarez when her terror was so great she would not leave the hotel. Tulsa reached out with one hand. She tried to move back, but he caught the square neck of the dress and ripped down. He tore out the entire front of it. What was left of the dress hung from one shoulder. He plucked it off and tore away the wisps of nylon. She tried to cover herself and then let her hands drop slowly to her sides. Some of the courage was gone, some of the spirit. She kept her chin up, her eyes fixed on Tulsa, but her mouth trembled.

Benny made a grunt of appreciation. Tulsa said, "You look maybe a little better than I guessed, Mrs. Danton. Scared?"

"What . . . what are you going to do?"

"Right now? Get a drink. You stand right there, Mrs. Danton. Hell, you're a lot better than a pinup. More real. You want a drink?"

"No."

"Seriously, Mrs. Danton, that's the only break I'm giving you. Harry wouldn't like me doing this, giving you a drink. You want to know how it goes? You got yourself killed. When you and Lloyd darling were twenty miles outside of Oasis Springs, you were a dead girl. Didn't you know?"

"Can't you . . ."

"Not with Harry giving the orders, I can't. You're just as dead as Lloyd darling. You're standing there dead. Now you want a drink?"

Her eyes were staring. She looked at Lloyd and through him. "Yes," she whispered.

Benny brought Tulsa the glass and the bottle he had just opened. Tulsa poured the glass more than half full of tequila. She sipped it. Lloyd stared at Valerez. The man looked uncomfortable, embarrassed. Benny glanced at Sylvia greedily.

"Hurry it up," Tulsa said.

She gulped and coughed and gulped again. Her face looked dulled, her eyes glazed, her complexion grayish. There was sweat on her face and shoulders and breasts. She finished the last of the tequila. Tulsa took the glass from her, threw it to Benny. Benny caught it deftly. Tulsa pushed the girl back into the bedroom and closed the door behind the two of them.

Lloyd stared incredulously, with a sick horror, at the closed bedroom door. He shut his eyes hard upon the scene in his mind, but he could not blot it out. Benny pulled his chair—the chair with Lloyd in it—over to the table.

"Join the party," Benny said cheerfully. "You keep sitting around in corners with your mouth shut, people won't like you. You know how to play gin, Giz? Good! You got some competition." Benny slapped the cards on the table and fanned them. He leaned close to Lloyd, winked in a jovial, insinuating way, jerked his thumb toward the closed bedroom door and said, "Little card game keeps a fella's mind off stuff and things. My deal."

Benny dealt deftly, picked up his hands, brows knotted, lips moving as he read off his cards to himself. The radio had been tuned low, so low the hillbilly music from Texas was but barely audible. Lloyd looked at Benny and recognized the expression on his face. It was the same expression he had seen so many times when Benny sat reading one of his comic books. Benny specialized in the fantasy comic books, full of slimed monsters, leggy girls in space suits, young scientist heroes and death rays. Lloyd remembered all the times he had forced himself to endure patiently Benny's retelling of one of the plots, little squat Benny with his lumpy clown face, wriggling with intensity, exuding a fine spray of spittle when he came to the most dramatic parts. He had heard that Benny Bernholz was one of Harry Danton's most reliable and efficient hoodlums, but that did not seem credible. He remembered how Benny had become fascinated with the way the landscape architects were turning the raw land around the Hotel Green Oasis into a tropical garden, how he annoyed the workmen with countless questions. Later, Harry Danton had let Benny take sole responsibility for a large formal flower bed to the east of the hotel, between the Olympic pool and the Copper Casino. Benny haunted the garden supply store down in the village of Oasis Springs, had struggled through the terminology of dozens of catalogues. The flower bed had been a masterpiece. Benny had made an event out of each new bloom, a disaster out of any hint of blight. No tourist could take a photograph of the large flower bed without Benny quickly sidling into the scene, chest inflated, carefully casual, his lesser version of a Durante nose as red as his bald spot from the long hours in the desert sun.

It was easier to picture Tulsa in the role of hired assassin, yet even that had not seemed plausible a thousand years ago when he and Tulsa had played gin at odd moments, when he and Tulsa had gone out into the big kitchens when the skeleton night staff was on and had made the thick sandwiches of tongue and imported cheese and rare roast beef. Tulsa's last name was Haynes, and he was from Oklahoma and he was half Indian. His shoulders were so broad that at a distance he looked much shorter than his six feet. Lloyd had seen him, on a drunken wager, plant his feet, stand with his back to the hood, squat so he could grasp the bumper, and lift the front wheels of a Buick clear of the ground.

Lloyd had felt he was close to them, friendly with them. In the chain of command, as hotel manager, he was their superior. Almost, but not quite. Harry Danton had said, "Use the boys when you can, Lloyd. I'd rather have you keeping them busy than have Charlie trying to use them." Charlie Bliss was in charge of the gambling end and worked with Harry Danton on the entertainment.

But, with both Benny and Tulsa, there was a curious reserve he could not penetrate. He was not quite one of the club. Sometimes he felt they came very close to patronizing him. Benny and Tulsa would go off on unexplained missions, sometimes alone, sometimes together, for as long as two weeks, though usually for only a day or two. Once when Tulsa came back, Lloyd made the mistake of asking him where he had been. Tulsa looked at him without any expression and said, "I've been to London to see the queen." Lloyd didn't ask again. He knew that the Hotel Green Oasis was but one phase of Harry Danton's operations, and that for various reasons Harry had chosen it as his headquarters. There were often special guests who had to be given rooms, the best suites, regardless of the reservation picture. These men generally drank and ate in their suites, spent hours in conferences with Harry, and seldom appeared in the Copper Casino. One of them, a small grey man without hair, eyebrows or lashes, registered often as J. Baron. Harry Danton treated him with respect bordering on servility, and had instructed Lloyd to see personally that Mr. Baron received top service. Each time Baron was in the house, Charlie Bliss had to move a silver dollar slot up to his suite after having a mechanic drop the 60-40 odds back to 50-50.

He had known Benny and known Tulsa, and now he knew that he had not known them at all, nor had he known Harry Danton. These men had been outside the range of his experience, and beyond his ability to project an awareness of evil. But now he had a new appreciation of them. Now he had seen them on the job. Now he knew their value to Harry. Any man without heart or conscience, with only ruthlessness and cruelty, can be invaluable to the Harry Dantons.

Lloyd sat tied in the chair. The script was wrong. There were always the good guys and the bad guys. And the beautiful woman. Lloyd had known all his life that he was one of the good guys. That made it simple, because then you always knew how it came out. The good guy and the beautiful girl would always get into one hell of a mess, but something always happened just at the very last minute, just when they both seemed doomed. Something happened. The bonds were worked loose, and you felled the bad guys with a chair. Or the cops came. Or the cavalry. It usually happened just when they were getting set to torture you. But something was wrong with this script and they went right ahead and did it. It didn't happen in the nick of time. The nick of time went right on by while you screamed and screamed onto a bloody towel. And always the beautiful girl was threatened by a fate worse than death. And they never quite got to her. They made some error in timing, or they left a gun around loose. But this nick of time went right on by too. So you sat and watched a game of rummy and you looked hard at the cards in Benny's hand and the cards he drew so you could take your mind away from the crawling horrors behind a locked door.

Tulsa came out of the bedroom, buckling his belt. He left the door open. He looked casually at Lloyd, and stood behind Benny, looking down into his hand. Benny drew the ten of spades, went down with four and caught Valerez with twenty-three count.

"Take it from here," Benny said. "It's no blitz. He lucked out on me two hands ago." He got up and Tulsa took his chair. "How is it, Tuls?" he asked.

"She ain't what anybody'd call cooperative," Tulsa said.

"Me, I got enough cooperation for two." He swaggered over to the door, hitching his pants up. He knocked on the door frame and cooed, "Oh darling! Are you decent?"

He went in and shut the door. Tulsa and Valerez played cards. They drank tequila. Lloyd saw a mosquito land on Tulsa's shoulder. The muscles quivered like the hide of a horse and the insect whined away. He looked at Tulsa's thick brown neck and thought of knives. Valerez went gin three times in a row and Tulsa scowled with annoyance. As far as the two men were concerned, Lloyd did not seem to exist. Benny came out, burlesquing extreme exhaustion. He kibitzed until the game was finished. Then Valerez looked inquiringly at Tulsa.

"Go ahead," Tulsa said. He went quickly. When the door had closed behind him, Benny said, "They like to get hold of a white woman. He'd like it better if she was blonde."

"Was she still crying?" Tulsa asked.

"No. She's like a zombie. Your deal, Tuls. Say, there's a pretty smart operator, that spic."

"He found 'em quick."

"You don't give me any more cards than he did. Want to make this a half buck a point?"

"Sure. After this game."

"Wise guy," Benny muttered and put down a cold hand for gin.

Valerez came out, pulled another chair over, and combed his hair straight back with a small green comb. He gave Lloyd a quick nervous glance. They started a three-handed game at higher stakes. They played for an hour. Tulsa went back into the bedroom. After he came out, Benny went in. Then he came hurrying right back out, rigid with indignation.

"Chrissake, Tuls. She's dead! You killed her! What the hell did you do? Her face is all dark like."

Tulsa flexed one big hand in a descriptive gesture.

"What the hell for?" Benny demanded.

"You want to say goodby or something? I said goodby, for you and me and Giz and Harry and Lloyd darling and all the folks back home."

Benny sat down and looked petulantly at Tulsa. "You know, sometimes you give me the God damn creeps, you thick-headed Indian."

"You want in the game or don't you?"

Benny sighed. "So deal me in. How much longer we got?"

Tulsa looked at his watch. "An hour."

"Want I should get a fresh bottle outa the car?"

"No more drinks."

The gag made Lloyd's jaws ache. He watched the three of them and thought of all the ways he could kill them, all the ways he would enjoy. The chair back cut into his upper arms. His arms were numb from there on down.

Finally Tulsa said, "Go put clothes on her, Benny."

"Hey, Tuls! Honest! I can't touch nothing like that."

Tulsa put his cards down. "She's gotta have clothes on. So go dress her. Now!"

Benny mumbled, whined but obeyed. He came to the bedroom door and said in a surly voice, "So she's dressed. Now what?"

"Now put her in the Pontiac."

"She's too heavy."

Tulsa cursed and got up. Lloyd watched him carry her out of the bedroom. He got one look at her dead face. Her right eye had been hammered shut. It was knotted like blue grapes.

And then there had been the ride up out of the night of the valley into the dawn of the mountains.

He lay on his back and the small leaves of the brush made a pattern against the stars. The wind changed. A whisper of breeze carried the scent of decay to his nostrils. He heard a dog bark, very far away. The stream made a hurrying sound close by. A few insects made a thin and endless screaming.

Tulsa, Benny, Valerez, Harry. I'll get out of here. Somehow I'll get out of here.

3

From then on there was no coherence to thought or memory. There was blazing sun, a memory of the car, crumpled as though it had been wadded in a fist, and beginning to rust. There was a pasty mess in a hub cap and he tried to swallow it. There were the birds waiting. Then he burned, and he made his croaking shouts and he listened for the inhuman echo. There was rain, and pain, and the heat of fever, and all kinds of curious things that came to him, Harry stepping carefully over the stones, Sylvia clinging to his arm, both of them smiling as they came toward him, and on their shoulders were perched the black vultures, riding easily there.

Then he was face down and something carried him along, lurching with him, something with shaggy brown hair and small hooves. Much later there was a dark and smoky place and hard hands holding him down as he screamed and screamed.

Everything was twisted and distorted, without continuity or meaningfulness—bright flashes and long patches of blackness. It was like a storm that passed over and through him and faded away down a valley.

By turning his head to the left he could see the bright irregular oblong of the door, the sunlight outside. He lay on a rustling softness, close to the floor, and the floor was of packed dirt. He liked to look out. He could see the side of a hill, and a wedge of sky. The hill was cultivated. Sometimes he could see people working in that incredibly steep field.

When the light was right, when it was late in the day, the sun walked slowly in across the dirt floor. It never quite reached him. Before it reached him, the sun dropped behind a mountain. When it was closest he could reach out and touch the edge of the sunlight. It was a long time before he had strength to do that. His hands were too heavy to lift. When the light was strongest, he often looked at his hands. They were pale and trembling and skeletal. His wrists were like stalks. The right palm was deeply scarred. The left wrist was lumpy, and had but limited movement. The fingers worked. The wrist would bend forward, but he could not move it from side to side.

He often felt of his face. His lower jaw was tied in place. It felt like a piece of rawhide that passed under his chin, over the top of his head. There was no familiarity in the contours under his fingertips. He was heavily bearded, yet there were shiny places where the beard did not grow. His nose felt like a withered button, and the left side of his face felt strangely hollow. His tongue explored the splintered stubs of teeth, finding the sharp places, lingering there.

At night six of them slept in the small square room and an adjoining room. They cooked there, on a sheet of metal over charcoal. There was an old lantern lighted only on special occasions. Smoke found its own way out a hole in the thatched roof. Sometimes, when the wind was wrong, they all coughed and choked. It seemed a long time before he could tell them apart clearly, or isolate their names out of the babble of conversation. For a long time he had not had the energy to try, but as the life trickled slowly back into him, and as his mind came alive, he began to listen for the names, try to figure out the relationships, try to pick up words and phrases of their conversation. There were three children, three boys. Pepe was about twelve, Armandito about eight, Felipe about six. They were happy children, with wide brown almost identical faces. They would often come and look down upon him with solemn unwinking curiosity.

The man of the house was named Armando, a squat brown man with a look of leathery toughness, a shock of startlingly white hair. His woman, the mother of the boys, was Concha who was perhaps thirty, perhaps twenty years younger than Armando, a placid heavy woman who sometimes fed him, spooning soups and thick pastes through the gap where teeth had been, holding him up gently when she held the pottery cup of cold water to his lips, washing his body with brusque efficiency in which there was a leavening of tenderness.

Usually it was the girl who took care of him. Her name was Isabella, and often they called her 'Bella or 'Bellita. She seemed to be seventeen or eighteen, a sturdy girl with a broad brown face in which he saw a family resemblance to the three boys, with black thick brows, black braided hair coarse and shiny as the tail hair of a black horse. She came to feed him and care for his needs during the day when the others worked, came to him smelling of sun and the fields and of sweat, impersonally gentle, sometimes crooning to him with the reassuring sounds you make to a small child. He knew she was not directly of this family, yet somehow related. She called Concha Tia, and Armando Tio. It was Isabella who taught the small boys. She made them drone lessons in unison, and she made them draw letters in the packed dirt outside the room with a pointed stick.

Other people often came to the rooms and there was much talk. And much laughter. And often music and singing. These were poor people, he knew. They worked very hard. Their life had a certain cadence of love. Many times other women, two or three, would come to visit Concha. They would bring flat stones and stone rollers and they would sit for tireless hours on the floor, cross-legged, grinding corn. With water and lime water they would turn the white powder into a paste, then slap it into tortillas. The slapping sounds merged with the sun and the sleepy afternoon, and their light quick voices as they worked and talked.

They were a clean people. He could hear the sound of falling water not far away. They used a coarse soap. Isabella sometimes wore her braids in coronet fashion. Other times the two long braids dangled. Sometimes when she bent over him, one of the coarse gleaming ropes would fall across his face, smelling of sun and freshness and the strong soap. There were goats that sometimes came and peered in at the door. When the wary scrawny chickens wandered in, Concha would flap her skirts and chase them out.

For a long time he was aware only of such a complete weariness, such an utter exhaustion, that he could not do anything for himself, nor could he concentrate long on what went on around him. His attention span was as short as that of a small child, and he slept often. He did not try to speak. In sleep he did not dream.

Then, when the days were very warm, he began to take an interest in things around him, and began to do more for himself. When he hitched himself up into a half-sitting position and reached for the bowl, Isabella let him feed himself until, half-way through, his hands and arms became too weary. It was then that he began to exercise as he lay there, working the muscles of arms and legs, shoulders, back and belly, bringing the strength slowly back. And he began to try to say some of the words he heard. Because of the tied jaw, his articulation was both guttural and hissing, but he could say "Gracias" to them so they could understand it and smile at him and beam very proudly. He listened when they talked, and though he began to understand a phrase here and there, he could not follow any conversation.

It was Isabella during one day of rain who took the initiative. She sat crosslegged by his pallet, expression earnest, voice taking on the same flavor of authority she used when she taught the small boys. She pointed to her head and said, "Cabeza," then waited until he repeated it in his curious voice. Then a heavy braid in her hand. "Pelo." Then, "Pelo negro." And then the words for hand, foot, arm, eye, nose, mouth, tongue, teeth, neck, fingers, knee, ear, stomach, heart. Then, mutely, she pointed at each object in turn. He missed two out of the list the first time, made a perfect score the second time. She smiled broadly and with pleasure at him.

It was either that day or the next, when they were away that he managed to crawl through the doorway, and, shaking with the effort, brace his back against the adobe wall and soak up the sunlight. He looked at the hills, and down the slope of the valley. He saw the other huts with their thatched roofs. Each was built into the living hillside, so that they were half hut, half cave. He saw the sparkling fall of water, a stream that came from a cleft in the rock and fell ten feet, shining like silver, a column thick as a man's body, sending up a mist that made a permanent rainbow. He looked at the wide blue of the sky and looked down at his outstretched legs. He guessed he could not weigh more than a hundred and twenty pounds. In full health he had carried a hundred and eighty pounds on his six-foot, two-inch frame, a man of heavy bone structure and quick lithe muscles. Tears of weakness ran from his eyes into the heavy mat of ginger beard.

They made exclamations of wonder when they returned, and they helped him back to the pallet. After that there were lessons each day. As the words and ideas became more abstract, Isabella was forced to act them out. She would sit for a time, frowning at the wall, then leap up and, in pantomime, create the meaning for the word she taught him. He listened to them and could not understand them and thought he would never learn the language. It changed for him, suddenly and dramatically one evening. They sat outside in moonlight and they were talking and he was making no particular effort to understand them. And, as though some hidden switch in his mind had been turned on, he found that he could understand. They spoke of a Roberto and whether it was time for him to go to Talascatan again, and what objects he should bring back from the village. He sat up in the darkness and he was very excited. He listened. He missed many words, but he could follow all they said. And he could understand words he had not realized he knew. Some of them had slipped into his mind during the early weeks when he was close to death, he decided.

From then on he and Isabella began to speak together in simple sentences. When the others understood they should go slowly, he could converse with them too. He became pleased with his own increasing proficiency. One afternoon Armando brought a man back with him. Lloyd was sitting outside. They squatted on either side of him, fingered the bound jaw, argued violently. Armando, Lloyd understood, felt that the jaw was now sufficiently healed, that enough time had passed. The other man, Rosario, claimed that when a man had been very ill, the bones healed more slowly. Armando said heatedly that if it was bound much longer, it would no longer work. In the end they cut the strip of leather. It had worked itself into the flesh of the underside of his jaw and had to be pulled free gently. Both men were delighted when Lloyd thanked them with an articulation he could not previously manage. There had been a considerable atrophy of the muscles. When he sat upright his lower jaw, after a period of time, tended to sag. He could not chew at first, and later, when the muscles had regained strength, he could only chew far back on the grinding molars.

The sun had moved and the nights began to be chilly. When he asked, Isabella told him it was the seventeenth day of October. It shocked him to learn how many months had gone by. Five months and eight days since he had gone over the cliff. He walked for the first time that day, sweating with effort, leaning heavily on the sturdy shoulders of Isabella, walking ten steps while she grinned encouragement. His left ankle was very stiff, yet not frozen in place. He could move it, but only at the expense of grating pain. For three days it was too swollen to attempt walking again. Soon he could walk without help, but not far. He felt too tall, teetering and fragile, like a man on a tightrope. Appetite and strength improved and he began to put on weight more rapidly.

As yet, with any of them, there had been no talk of past or future. On a day colder than any that had gone before, Isabella came to him with a strange shyness. She held something out to him and said, "Is it permitted to wear this?"

He took it from her and it took long moments to identify it. It came from another life, a life before this one. He saw that it was one of Sylvia's sweaters, cashmere in a dark red, with a design in white at the throat.

Holding it, he said, "Is there more clothing?"

"Yes. For you and for her. A lot of it."

"It is more cold now. You and Concha must take her clothing and use it. She is dead."

"I know. What was her name?"

"Sylvia. And the other clothing, the boys must use what can be fitted to them. You have . . . shared all you have with me. I will share with you."

She thanked him. She wore Sylvia's clothing. The skirts were too long. They fit at the waist, but were tight over Isabella's heavier hips. She was shy at first, and then pleased with herself. Armando self-consciously wore one of Lloyd's tweed jackets. It fit across the shoulders, but came almost to his knees.

He said one day to Isabella, "How did I come here?"

She looked at him and finally nodded. "It is time to talk. I will tell my uncle."

There was a conference that evening. Goat skin covered the doorway, a protection against the chill of the nights. Now, each night, the cook fire was left burning. The lantern was lighted on this special occasion. The boys were sent into the adjoining room. Armando, Concha, Isabella, the man named Roberto, and Lloyd sat around the lantern.

"We must talk," Armando said. And he reached over and handed Lloyd an object which Lloyd recognized as his own wallet. Lloyd halted himself just in time before looking in it. He sensed that would be rude. He put it casually aside and said, "Thank you."

"It contains thirty-four American dollars and eleven hundred and ten pesos. It is a great deal of money," Armando said.

But not enough, Lloyd thought, even to tempt Tulsa or Benny to take it. That was part of the window dressing if the accident was discovered. "I thank you for saving it for me."

Armando nodded gravely. He told the story. When it was Roberto's turn, he took over. They both spoke slowly for Lloyd's sake. Roberto had been gathering charcoal after a mountain fire. He had his two burros with him. He had looked down into a valley and seen a glint of metal. All the way home he had wondered about it, and, two days later, had gone down into the valley with one burro. He had found the Señor Lloyd in madness, very close to death. Roberto had waited for death to come, but it did not. Finally he had placed the Señor Lloyd on the burro and had brought him back to this place. He did not die on the seven hour trip as Roberto had expected. They were mountain people here, accustomed to the breaking of bones and the fixing of bones. They fixed the jaw and the wrist and the ankle, not as well as a doctor could do it, but as well as they could. The fever was very bad. He was like a bed of coals. They gave him remedies and waited for him to die. It was a curious problem. If the Señor Lloyd should die, then the money and the things from the automobile would properly belong to Roberto, and to Armando who was his cousin. This was fair because it had been Armando who, hearing Roberto's story, had urged him to go back to the valley. But it was not permitted to kill the Señor Lloyd. They were not murderers in this valley, except for a true cause, and to make profit was not a true cause. It was equally murder to neglect a man's wounds. The honorable thing was to care for the Señor Lloyd. If he died, there would be no question of taking his money and possessions. If he lived, such a thing could not be done. They were not thieves in this valley. The Señor Lloyd had lived and now was stronger each day. When the time came, they would bind his eyes and Roberto would take him to a place where he could easily walk to the village of Talascatan. It was regrettable the binding of the eyes was necessary, but a vote had been taken, and though it would appear the Señor Lloyd had reasons for being grateful, it was best that no one should worry about such a matter.

And now, in fairness, it should be explained why no doctor was brought to the Señor Lloyd. There are twenty-eight persons in this valley, counting the children. There was political trouble in the village of Pinal Blanco, a village which is two villages beyond Talascatan. There was a tax matter and killing, and powerful enemies made. A price was placed on the heads of certain men. The choice was to become bandits, or live in a hidden place in peace. They were not thieves, nor murderers. This is a hidden valley. The trail is very difficult. Roberto, who is not wanted by the law, goes to Talascatan for their needs. It is a way to live in peace, but there are difficulties. No doctor, no schools, no church. But that is better than being a bandit, no?

Armando said, into the silence, "And you have strong enemies too, Señor Lloyd."

It was statement, not question. They would have seen the burns on chest and feet. They had been frank, and expected an equal frankness.

"They are enemies from my country. They followed me here. They found me at a hotel in Talascatan. They strangled the woman, put us in my car and pushed us over the edge."

There was a gasp of horror and interest. "I do not know how it is you live," Armando said.

"They believe me dead."

Armando fingered his chin. "If they did this thing, why did they not take your money?" he said suspiciously.

"They took money. They took so much money, the little they left me was not of importance."

"What will you do?"

"When I am strong, I will leave here and I will go back to my country and I will kill them."

Armando and Roberto nodded.

"There are four of them," Lloyd said.

Roberto said, "It is miraculous that a man as badly broken could raise up such a great pile of stones over the body of the woman."

"So the zopilotes would not have her body," Lloyd said. "They angered me."

"If that is the quality of your anger," Roberto said, "when you are in health you can kill them with your hands."

"All but one. With him I am a child."

"Then use the knife."

He looked at them and he knew he had not yet matched their honesty, nor repaid them with frankness for all they had done for him. He groped for words, knowing he would have difficulty with abstract ideas.

"I will tell you this thing. It is about the money and the woman. The thing I did was not honorable."

Armando said, "It is not necessary for you to tell."

"I feel it is necessary." He found himself looking at Isabella. She was looking down at her clasped hands. "The money and the woman. They were not mine. I took them. I was followed." He looked around at impassive faces. "But a thing cannot be black or white. I was a thief when I took the money, but that money had been stolen from others. I was a thief when I took the woman, but she was gentle and unhappy and often beaten. She asked me to take her away, and I wished to give her happiness. The men found us. My actions were not honorable, perhaps. But their actions were the actions of animals. With me and with the woman. Most of all with the woman, before one of them killed her. That is why it is necessary to kill them. I will not be a man again until that is done."

It was not something he could have said in his own land in his own tongue without feeling ridiculously melodramatic. And he wondered whether the need to kill would have been as understandable even to himself in another place and time. Yet here it was perfectly clear, and he could see that Armando and Roberto accepted it. Here there was no talk of the futility of revenge. This was a mission of honor.

After a long silence Armando reached his hand over and shook hands with Lloyd in American fashion. "It is good you have explained," he said. Lloyd felt the lantern heat on the underside of his wrist.

When his hand was released, he opened the wallet and took out the pesos. He held them for a moment, then turned and placed them in Concha's ample lap. "Many things are needed. This is not a payment. It is a gift. I wish, with your permission, Armando, to remain here until I am truly strong. When I can work, I will do so. With the money Roberto can buy things in the village for the good of all. More warm clothing for children is needed, more serapes for men, rebosas for women, blankets."

Concha touched the money, looked shyly at Armando. He nodded. "Mil gracias," she said. "It is cold here in the winter months."

Roberto left and came back proudly with a large bottle of mescal. The earthenware cups were gotten out. The drink tasted like varnish and sulphuric acid and had an impact like an unexpected blow on the head. Rosario arrived with battered guitar. There was singing and dancing. More people arrived until Lloyd was willing to swear the entire community of twenty-eight had gathered in the small room. He sat on the pallet, back against the wall, grinning and watching and beating time, drinking whenever anybody thought to pour something into his cup. Eleven hundred pesos was a little over ninety dollars. It merited a fiesta.

Isabella came and sat beside him, flushed and moist with the effort of dancing. She sipped from his cup. He took her hand. She tried to tug it away but he held it. She sat rigidly then, face half turned away.

"Do you care much," he said, "about the stolen money and the stolen woman?"

"Was she beautiful?" The question was small, almost lost in the din.

"To some, perhaps."

"To you?"

"For a time."

That seemed to satisfy her.

"Where are your people, Isabella?"

"Here."

"I mean your father and your mother, sisters, brothers."

She spoke casually. "Oh, they are dead. In all the killing, in Pinal Blanco. My father was a leader. The leader. The brother of Armando. We thought our party was the stronger, and so we were careless. They came in the night, to the houses of all the ones of our party and perhaps forty were killed that night, and many houses burned. It was a village of one hundred and fifty. There had been trouble for many many years, before I was born. My father and my mother and my brother and two younger sisters died. We are a cruel people. When the trouble is bad, even the little ones die. I received this. Mire!"

She pulled up her skirt, pulled it high up her thigh, exposing the scar on the outside of her thigh, a long puckered white scar. She pushed her skirt down.

"You do not seem sad."

"I am very sad when I think of it, Lloyd. But I do not often think of it. Our house was almost the best in the village."

"How long ago was it?"

"I had thirteen years. It was five years ago."

"Could you go back now?"

She stared at him in wonder. "Go back there? The daughter of Emiliano Calderon y Vega? The only child of the leader! I would not live out one night."

"I don't understand."

"Listen to me. It is very simple. There are twenty-eight here. One day, with luck, there will be a hundred. Many of those will be young strong men. What if some of those young strong men were my sons? They would know what happened. I would tell them and they would know. They would be brave and strong and very angry, no?"

"It is more than possible."

"One day there will be careful plans. We will be strong then and we will go back. The men will go back. You do not know this country. Sometimes, for many years, for maybe a hundred years, there will be a war between villages. The police and the soldiers do not matter. It is a war. One time when I was little a thing happened between villages. On a day when the men were far away in the fields, the other men from the other village marched in and killed all. Every woman, child and old man. These are serious matters."

"Would . . . Armando and Roberto and Rosario do such a thing?"

"They would not care to. It is not a good thing. They would like it if we can be strong enough to go by night. But suppose we do not become strong enough? Suppose too much time passes. And there is an impatience. Then they could do the other. But I would not like it. I know many girls who are still there. But by now they have married."

"So you will marry and have sons and teach them to hate the people of Pinal Blanco?"

"I will not marry, Lloyd."

"Why not?"

"Look! Look at the dance! Do you see a young man? No. You see old men who have wives. You see little girls and boy children and some widows. The oldest boy child is Pepe. When he has sixteen years, I will have twenty-one. Such a marriage could be made, but when he has sixteen years there will be three girls who have fifteen and sixteen years. Anyway, he is my nephew. No, I shall be Tia. I shall be aunt to everyone, and teach small ones because I did go to school, but not enough, not long enough. One day I would have gone to the universidad, and I would have been a respected teacher."

"Suppose your people can kill them and drive them away, and take the village. Then one day could they not come back in strength and do the same?"

"It is possible."

"But does it have meaning?"

She took the cup from him. "You are un poco borracho, Lloydito. What is meaning? Like an addition of sums. It is a matter of honor. You go to kill because you must, no?"

"Yes."

"You kill and you are once again a man in your heart. And you live as a man for one year and then a friend of the ones you killed kills you. Possible, also?"

"Yes."

"And you say it is of no meaning. But what of that year of walking like a man, Lloydito? Is that of no meaning? Estupido! If it were a month only. Or a week. Or even a moment. Then is not that a moment of truth?"

"I do not know."

"You do not know! I will tell you one thing. What if you have said it in your mind, I will not go and kill them? What if you have said it in your mind it is a matter too difficult and too dangerous. I live. I am lucky. I will forget them and I will live. Then what are you? An animal who hides in a small place. Can you walk on your legs? Can you look at a woman? Can you drink with men and laugh with men? No! There is the look of fear. There is the apology to everyone. Now you are a man because you know what is necessary for you to do and you know you will do it. It is a satisfaction in you. I tell you this thing. You live now because it was that necessary thing in your mind to give you strength. Do you not see strength here, with my people? What would happen to us if we say we have too much fear, we will never go back? Would we fight to live in this difficult place? No. We would all of us, sneak away. To strange villages far away, with doctors and schools and churches, and we would be strangers there. Never could we look into the eyes of another. Our men would be castrated by fear. Our women could take no pride in sons. It is a thing of living. It is a thing of honor. It is a thing to be understood, Lloydito." She hiccuped and said, "Lo siento mucho, pero creo 'stoy borracha también."

"I think I understand."

"There is a thing in a book, but it was long ago and I do not say it right. It is perhaps changed. I say it this way. For a man he must die on his feet because if he lives on his knees he is not a man. I have two bloods."

"I do not understand."

"Two bloods. De España y de las Aztecas. I know the history. Not much. I am ignorant. But I know this thing, Lloydito. The Spaniards were men, men in armor who came on little wooden ships from a far place and fought and won this country from many thousands of Indians. The Indians were brave and cruel and had much civilization, but not the things of war. So the two bloods are here, in me. With those two bloods, we have made ourselves free, just like your country. On each side the men were mucho hombre. On each side much honor and bravery, not so much with leaders, but with the little men. Now I will dance again. You think. In a little time I will bring more for the cup, no?"

He watched her dance with big-chested Roberto, her skirt swirling, braids snapping. She had kicked off her sandals and her bare feet stamped the floor in time to Rosario's guitar while the watchers clapped and snapped their fingers in a complicated flamenca rhythm.

Two bloods, he thought. Just a trace of the Spanish in the suggestion of the oval in her face, the hint of a hollowness in the cheeks, a slight arch to the black brows. She was the color of a penny. Not the fresh minted copper, but an old penny, paled into a fingered gold. Two bloods, and a code of blood. The sand of Mexico had quickly soaked up the steaming blood of honor for many years. A land of pride and of quick violence without mercy. Also a land of sullenness and the glorification of death. A land where they ate candy skulls, where brass marched in the funerals of children, where fireworks exploded under church pews on Christmas morning, a land where a baker from Monterrey, a bullfighter of neither nerve, grace nor talent, can finally achieve his goal of performing in the Plaza Mexico and filling its fifty-five thousand seats by a public proclamation of his intention to permit his first bull to kill him.

Though he was slightly drunk, his mind was working with a curious clarity, and he knew that in no other way could he have come as close to these people so quickly, could he have been privileged to see the working of their minds, the uncompromising qualities of their ethical standards. There had to be the language, even though he was as yet clumsy in it. And he had to have been there, helpless, for week after week, gaining through his helplessness a kind of acceptance. He knew his recovery had awed them. They knew of wounds and sickness, and they had an atavistic awareness of the closeness of death. Now they knew he had lived because he had to live, because there was a mission of honor involved. They could understand that. There was, in them, an instinctive knowledge of the interaction of mind and body. They knew of the bullfighter, one of the greatest ones, who, after escapes bordering on the miraculous, had finally been gored and, in fear, in humiliation, in superstitious terror, had looked at his own blood and had said, "I die," and had died of a horn wound not superficial, yet not nearly grave enough to cause death.

These people had stood atop pyramids at dawn and with an obsidian knife cut the living heart from an enemy, holding it up toward the rising sun, still pulsing in the hand of the priest. And, on the other side of the blood, they had stood bound in fire and died without scream or terror.

He watched them and felt his own blood was watery, his emotions pallid, all his angers merely spite, all his loves like spun sugar, all his juices like thin gruel.

Finally, wearied, he slept with his face to the wall, slept through the dancing and the singing and the time of the telling of stories that came later and lasted until the most distant peaks, the highest ones to the west, were touched with the first fire-glow of morning.

Soon he was able to walk to the other huts. There were eight altogether, as well as some outbuildings for storage. When he knew where the others lived, it was much easier to remember names and to sort out the confusing relationships. No one seemed unwilling to talk of the night of death and terror five years before. All told of miraculous escape, and he guessed that the difficulties of each individual escape had been enhanced in each retelling. Armando and Concha had, he thought, escaped as a family, with less loss than others. Then he learned that Armando's wife, who had been older, and grown sons and their wives and children had perished. Concha had lost her husband and one child, but had saved the two elder boys and had given birth to Felipe on the way to the valley.

When he learned that, he asked Rosario how Armando and Concha had been able to marry. Rosario thought that a great joke. He said that Roberto, who could read, had read what seemed to be an appropriate passage from the holy book and had, in the name of the exiles from Pinal Blanco, pronounced them man and wife. He asked Rosario what was funny and it took him some time to understand Rosario's explanation. It seemed that Concha had not been married before. True, she had lived with a man and called him husband and he called her wife, and the children had taken the proper name from such a union, but really there were very few couples in Pinal Blanco who had been married. You see, the priest came for one mass very late each Sunday, and he was always in a hurry. A civil wedding was possible if one cared to travel by bus all the way to Zimapan, but the buses did not run often, and it was expensive. The priest would marry, but at a fee of ninety pesos, and that was far beyond the reach of most couples. So it happened that by the time a couple had the money and the chance to be married, there were children to be cared for, and it was odd to go with one's children to be married, and anyway the situation was accepted by the others, so few bothered. And, he said, it was the same in all the remote villages of Mexico. Here, in the valley, marriage was easy and very cheap. Yes, the Mayor of Pinal Blanco could have performed marriages, but Rosario could remember five mayors and not one of them ever acquired the necessary forms, nor could they have completed them had they done so.

Each day he forced himself to walk farther, working the stiffness out of his foot, limbering the long muscles of the thighs. Constant washings, accomplished by beating the clothing against the stones of the stream, had turned his clothes to rags, and so he adopted the dress of the others.

At times he was discouraged at his own slow progress. December came, and in that cold month many things of importance happened to him.

4

In the valley, no matter how low the temperature, everyone in the settlement bathed in the clear cold water that came down from the cleft in the cliff face. Winter or summer, the shock of the water was considerable, both in weight and coldness. The first few times Lloyd had bathed there, Armando had gone with him to see that he came to no harm. A single fence of thatch protected the bather from the patient stares of those waiting to bathe, yet offered no protection against the curiosity of any of the women who might be washing clothes downstream from the bathing place.

When he first stepped under the stream it promptly knocked him down, and Armando pulled him, chilled, thrashing and sputtering, out of the turbulence of the pool carved out by the falling water. Soon he had become used to the force and weight of it, accustomed to its coldness, almost indifferent to the discomfort of washing himself with the harsh soap, drying his body on the rough scratchy texture of the serape before pulling on his trousers. Earlier he had been ashamed of the flaccid whiteness of his spindly body, the bones like an illustration in anatomy, and he knew that the women who washed clothing looked up the slope and marveled at the whiteness and the frailty. But even after the weather became cold, one could toast in the sun in a protected spot. He had found a niche in the rocks far from the huts and he spent time there when the sun was highest. He had always taken a tan easily, and in this clear air he took a deep tan. For a long time he had been spindly, knobby, under the waterfall, but at least tanned. Now he was filling out, and without softness. He guessed he was at about a hundred and fifty, still much too lean for his height, but the webs of muscle were rebuilding.

On one day he stood drying his thick curl of ginger beard and his short brown hair on the serape. Concha had recently cut his hair with a pair of shears so primitive he felt she was pulling it out rather than cutting it. She objected to his desire for such shortness, but did as he wished, reluctantly. Now he wondered how he looked with the heavy untrimmed beard. As he thought of it, it seemed odd to him that he had felt no desire to see how he looked. He knew his face had been badly damaged, and it gave him a curious feeling to touch the strange shrunken nose. He had always wondered about a beard, and it had surprised him that it had come out such a reddish shade. Red mixed with yellow, so the final product was like a pale toffee.

He put on trousers and shirt, put his head through the slit of the serape, and tried to find a pool where his face would be mirrored. The water was all too turbulent. He found one place where there was a pool, but it was in continual agitation from the current near it. He built a small dam of rocks and mud and the pool became quiet. He looked into it. He looked for long unbelieving moments and then sank back on his haunches, sick at heart. He looked again, cautiously, and the mirrored image was the same. He sat beside the stream and put his face in his hands.

Lloyd Wescott had been a presentable man of twenty-nine. He realized suddenly that he was now thirty: the birthday had been in June, a month he had no memory of. Some women had called Lloyd Wescott handsome. He had been a man with a rather long face, a square jaw with a cleft in the chin, brows that jutted a bit, deepset eyes of a grey-blue shade, a long straight nose, slightly flattened at the tip. He had been a good athlete, he moved well. He liked people sincerely, and so his charm had not been forced. He had been very good at his work, and that had given him an air of confidence and self-respect. Sometimes he had felt, as everyone does, a definite dissatisfaction with his face when he looked in the mirror. It did not seem to reflect what he felt he looked like.

But this mirror showed him horror. He saw a man he had never known. The high forehead was burned dark bronze by the mountain sun. The tiny irregularities he had felt under his fingertips turned into a great triangular scar, whitish pink against the bronze. It started at the outside edge of his right eyebrow, moved irregularly up on a slant to the middle of his forehead, and then cut back up into his hair on the right side. At the point of entry of the scar, the hair was dead white.

The eyes were deeper than he had ever seen them, and they seemed to have the staring glow of madness. The entire end of the nose was gone, almost to the bridge. It was a sickening thing to look at. In spite of the concealment of the great bushy beard, he could see that the lower part of the face, under the beard, was distorted. In the nest of the beard, between scarred and parted lips, he saw the broken fragments of teeth.

It was then that he came to an understanding of the true courtesy of these people. Not even the children had given him any sign by which he could know that he was monstrously ugly.

When he went back to the hut, Isabella was alone there, sewing. She sensed that something was wrong and she put her work aside.

"What has happened?"

"I saw my face in the water. I saw ugliness. A monster."

"That is not true!"

"It is what I saw."

"It is not what I see. It is not what anyone here sees, Lloyd."

"It is what I see. It is in my mind and I can't get it out."

"It is not as bad as that."

He looked at her. "Roberto brought all the things from the car. There are some things of mine. A razor."

"No," she said.

"He did not find those things?"

"We have them. You should not take away the beard. The way you are, the beard is good."

"Without the beard I'd be so hideous not one of you could bear to look at me?"

Her dark eyes flashed then and she backed away from him. "Perhaps you should be pretty, like a girl?" She walked mincingly, patting her hair. "With a skin so soft and sweet, like goat's milk. Maybe you want to be in the movies? Señor Roberto Taylor, perhaps, with great white teeth like a graveyard."

"I know that—"

She stamped her foot, and now her eyes were blazing. "Estupido! You fell from a mountain. You fell on the great stones. Should God have come running to hold under you a great bed of feathers? You should be dead. Your face is marked by the nearness of death. Be a man. Stop being a girl child weeping over a pimple!"

She whirled and left the hut and the goat skins fell back into place. The light in the room came from the chimney hole in the thatch, and around the edges of the goat skins. He sat on his heels. The others often sat that way. He had practiced until he was almost as tireless as they were. After a long time he grinned, and knew the grin showed the splintered teeth. Vanity was what had caused the pain. So he could stop thinking of vanity. There was money. Fortunately, a great amount of money. Money could buy teeth and a new tip for the nose. Those were essentials, reasonably utilitarian. He traced the scar with his fingertips, the scar on his forehead. That one must have been a brute. Hit in the middle and laid the scalp right back.

And he remembered a man who pulped berries between his fingers and tried to push them past his fractured jaw and down his throat. What sort of face would that man have settled for?

He knew exactly what he had to do. He found Isabella. He stood tall in front of her, hands on his hips. He looked down at her and grinned his broken grin.

"Truly, I am of a stupendous ugliness."

She started to object and then understood and smiled back. "No man can claim more."

"I will begin a new work. I will rent my face to mothers all over Mexico to frighten disobedient children."

She made the usual automatic correction of his grammar and said, "You will have much work. It will be successful. Mexico will have only good children."

"For love, I will have a mask made. It will be the face of the Señor Roberto Taylor. Then young maidens can fall madly in love with me. I will have great success in that work, also."

"For me," she said, "that is not a needed thing."

"This face does not alarm you?"

"If it does, I have the privilege of closing my eyes, Lloydito. What work did you do? You have never told."

"I am sorry. That is a rudeness. I was a manager of hotels. One hotel at a time. I went to a school and learned what must be done, and then had a small job, and then a bigger one, and a bigger one."

"Ah, you were good at that work. And important."

"Good, but not important."

She gave him a brooding look. "This Sylvia, she lived in your hotel?"

"Yes. She was the wife of the owner."

"Then he was not a thief as you said?"

"I did not lie. The money was made by gambling. The gambling was dishonest."

"Oh. Was it a big hotel? With many rooms? With . . . twenty rooms?"

He laughed aloud. "The land of the hotel is almost as big as all of this valley. There was a great pool of water to swim in. There were many buildings. There are more than two hundred rooms."

"Truly, you are the greatest liar of all."

"It is the truth."

Her questions had brought back memories. The next morning he worked with Armando, helping to clear land that would be planted in the spring. They felled the trees, dragged and rolled them down into the valley. It was hard work and he tired quickly. He had to rest often. Though he protested, Armando would not let him work longer than a half day as yet. After he had eaten hugely of tortillas and beans, he went off to his protected place in the rocks, stripped, and stretched out on his serape. The basic honesty of these people was an insidious thing, he realized. When you were exposed to it long enough, you were forced to reexamine your own motives. And he knew it was time for self-analysis, to go back over all of the events leading up to his flight with Sylvia, and try to understand completely why he had been able to become thief and wife-stealer.

Lloyd Wescott first met Harry Danton in the late summer of 1963. Lloyd, at that time, had just been promoted to manager of a deluxe resort hotel on the coast of Maine north of Portland. He had turned twenty-seven that summer, and was trying very hard to both look and act older. It was an old hotel, with a regular clientele who had become so accustomed to the sedate ways of the previous manager that they tended to treat Lloyd as though he were a half step higher than a bell hop. This was the first season under new ownership, and the new owners hoped to attract new business. Lloyd, then working as assistant manager of a very large and successful summer hotel in the Adirondacks, and in the winter as assistant manager of a hotel in Jacksonville, Florida, owned by the same people, heard of the vacancy in Maine and applied for the job. He was thoroughly astonished when they hired him. He got to Maine six weeks before opening. A new pool and a new lounge were being constructed. He worked an estimated twenty-hour day for six weeks, lived through the first three days of the opening, and then went to bed for forty-eight hours.

His delicate mission was to attract younger people without alienating the old hands. The hotel had not been operating at capacity for several years because far too many of the elderly clientele had died, and too many had become unfit for travel.

In his greenness and in his eagerness to have a full house, he had taken several chances on mail reservations, trusting to his judgment and instinct, there being no time to check back. He approved a reservation for a one bedroom suite and a single on the same floor in the name of a Mr. Harry Danton of Detroit. Danton's letter was on creamy thirty pound bond. The letterhead said A and D Enterprises, Incorporated, and gave a Detroit address, two phone numbers, a cable code. The accompanying check for two hundred and fifty dollars was imprinted with the name of the corporation, had been made out on a checkwriter, and was signed by Harry A. Danton. Lloyd remembered fingering the bond paper, running a fingertip over the engraved letterhead, and saying, after checking the occupancy board, "Okay. Confirm it."

He then forgot it until the morning of August fifteenth. He got down to the front at eight fifteen. He had had to attend one of the guest parties the night before, but had managed to slip out early enough to get in six hours. He knew that if he could get through the house routine, the office routine and the kitchen routine early enough, he could catch a nap in the three to five lull.

Belter was the night man on the desk. He had twenty years of front experience and Lloyd respected his judgment.

"Morning, Stu. Check-ins?"

"A couple. The Durards. Old hands here. Two brat kids, but they tip the whole house. Another case where they'll want a personal welcome from the new manager."

"Tell Smitty to let me know when they come down for breakfast."

"The other one, I think, is a problem. I don't know how much, but a problem for sure."

"Ouch!"

"Harry Danton from Detroit."

Lloyd frowned, then snapped his fingers. "Suite and a single. Right?"

"Right. For about three weeks, he says."

"What's wrong?"

"You can smell money from here to there. He looks like maybe he runs a bank. I mean people might guess that about him. Not me. He's got eyes on him like looking down a gun sight at you. He's smartened up a lot, but the clothes are just a *little* bit wrong. And the way he talks is just a *little* bit wrong."

"You mean you know him?"

"No. I wouldn't have caught it from the name alone. But seeing him and adding the name to it, I ring me a far away bell, Lloyd. Mob stuff. Syndicate stuff. I've heard the name in that connection. Those people from the old days have gone very respectable, you know."

"If you're right, he isn't the type we're after. But maybe you're the only one who'll be able to tell, Stu."

Belter grinned. "About *him,* yes. But the item in the single is going to churn this place. Here's the sign-in. Miss Daintree West. About five nine. Really stacked. An accent right out of the five and dime. Blonde hair down to here. Black tight pants, green shirt, green shoes, green gloves to her elbows, mink stole. They came into Portland on a late flight and taxied out. While he registered, she stood right where you're standing, yawning and combing her hair. Finally she said, 'Jee-*zuzz,* Harry, snap it up! I'm pooped.' She's maybe twenty. He's maybe fifty. She's signed in as his secretary. If she can type, I'm old Dirty Thumb Gulick."

"So what do we do?"

"One thing, Lloyd, you don't do. You don't push him around. For solid procedure, I'd recommend you close your eyes and hope they go away."

It wasn't until late on the following afternoon that Lloyd had a chance to talk to Danton. He spotted them on the other side of the pool. Smitty had previously pointed them out in the dining room.

Danton wore a white silk sport shirt, navy blue shorts. He sat in a deck chair wearing dark glasses, reading. His legs were pink from the sun. The girl lay beside him on the pool apron, face up, plastic cups on her eyes, body greased. She wore a bikini that looked as though it were made of white satin. Lloyd had already heard about the bikini. The comments were not exactly complaints.

When Lloyd approached he saw that Danton was reading a racing form. When Lloyd said, "Mr. Danton?" Danton stuck the folded form under one hip and looked up.

"I'm Lloyd Wescott, the manager here. I'm just getting around to welcoming you aboard."

Danton took his hand and shook it briefly, making no attempt to get up. "Sit down a minute, Wescott. I got a couple things I want to kick around with you. Pull that chair over."

Lloyd had not intended to sit down. But there was a definite force and authority about the man. He had a round face, thick white hair, black brows. He took the sun glasses off. His eyes were small and of a vivid blue and they slanted down at the outside corners. His nose was slightly flattened at the bridge. He had a curious build. He was too tall and too wide for the round undersized head. His body had width without thickness, except for the small hard pod, the size of a half watermelon. He held his back very straight, and later, when Lloyd watched him move around, the straightness seemed more an indication of stiffness and a wary fragility than of a military bearing.

"How about a drink, Wescott?"

"Not right now, thanks."

"I'm ready. Daintree!" She grunted in a sleepy way. "Go get me another bourbon on the rocks."

"Jee-*zuzz,* Harry! Can'tcha see I'm—"

He interrupted her with such a hefty kick in the upper part of the thigh that it nearly rolled her over. When she popped up, gasping with outrage, he leaned toward her and said softly, "Go get the drink or go pack. And when I say move, get off your lazy butt next time."

"Okay, Harry. All *right.*"

She got up meekly and went off, limping slightly, rubbing the bruised hip. Harry turned quickly and caught an expression on Lloyd's face. "Ha! Shouldn't kick 'em, eh?"

"Only in private, Mr. Danton. Too many people watch for things like that."

"I get it. When I can get away I spend a lot of time in Miami. One time on the beach a friend of mine, name doesn't matter, got sore by the hotel pool. Busted his girl in the nose and threw her in. Busted his girl friend's girl friend in the nose and threw her in. Then busted his girl friend's girl friend's boy friend on the beak and heaved him in. You never see a busier lifeguard. Whole damn pool turned kinda pink. It cost him eighteen hundred bucks to get the three noses fixed. There was no beef."

"It's a little different here."

"It's a different crowd."

"Yes."

"Watching you last night. Saw you moving around like you were giving a hell of a big party. This place runs smooth."

"Thank you, Mr. Danton."

The girl brought the drink. He took it without thanks. She coiled languidly down onto the sun mattress, straightened the oiled and gleaming legs, recupped her eyes and sighed mightily to indicate her martyrdom.

"It's little things I guess. That little gal in the Dutch outfit coming around to the table all the time with that thing full of hot rolls. And on the breakfast tray this morning comes the Detroit paper. That shook me up."

"You'll get it every morning you're here. I have to be—"

"Hold it just a couple of minutes, Wescott. How big a staff you got?"

"Counting the gardeners, life guards and maintenance, a hundred and eleven."

"Runs a big nut then. Got any idea of the return on the investment?"

"No, I haven't."

"Here's what I want. I want to mouse around a little. Case the operation. I won't get in anybody's way."

"Why, Mr. Danton? This house isn't on the market."

"I wouldn't want this place. It's beat. I think I want to build me one."

"It's a quick easy way to go broke, they tell me."

"I'm in a lot of things. People can go broke in any one of them, Wescott. I don't, on account of always I get top people and give them their head. Can I look around a little?"

"Of course, Mr. Danton."

That was the beginning. Lloyd saw him after that in all parts of the house. Once he stood in an out-of-the-way corner of the main kitchen throughout the dinner hour. He spent time with the bell captain, with the housekeeper, at the reservation desk. Miss West checked out at the end of the first week. Danton said, "I sent her back. That one was all slob. I ask a friend who he knows wants a vacation. The trouble is this friend is all slob too so I get one with no more conversation than a rabbit and she acts like *she's* doing *me* a favor. Bet you're awful sorry she's gone."

The day Danton checked out, he asked Lloyd to come up and have a drink in the suite. He wasted no time. "How about coming in with me? One and a half times whatever you're getting, and a piece of the profit at the end of the year?"

"Where's your hotel?"

"In a lock box. Finish up here, then you go to work. Go look for a site and phone me when you find one.

You pick the architects and work with them. Then you live on the job while we're building, and then you open it up and run it. Only one catch. The site has got to be in Nevada. Think it over and phone me."

Lloyd talked it over with Stu Belter two days later. "It sounds too good to be true. What the hell does he know about me?"

"Don't kid yourself. Those boys use all the sources. I'll bet he knows how old you were when you took your first step."

"What do you think?"

"Don't ask me. Some of the boys have landed on their feet out there. Others have had a lot of heartache. You got to face the fact it's mostly mob money. And where there's gambling you get people in the house acting like maniacs. They run a heavy entertainment nut and you have to put up with high level tantrums. Maybe you could do it. Nothing seems to ruffle your feathers. You've got a trick of making the job look easy. The way it looks to me, it's rich out there and there's a lot of gloss but all the same it's a little shabby."

"If I take it, would you come out later on?"

"Good God, no! When Rosie fastens herself to a slot machine, you can't pry her off with a tire iron. Right now I'm trying to support a family and a horse room. She's incurable."

A week later a gift arrived from New York, a slender dull silver cigarette case in good taste, with his initials L. T. W. engraved on one corner. Danton's card was enclosed. Belter said it looked like platinum. Lloyd told him he was crazy. The next time he was in Portland he had a jeweler look at it. It was platinum, with an estimated retail value of four hundred dollars.

That week he landed a winter job in New Orleans and wrote Danton, thanking him for the cigarette case and telling him he had decided against taking the job he had offered.

He forgot all about Danton until March of 1964 when he got a call that a man wanted to see him in the men's bar. The New Orleans job was a dog. The new owner, a small fussy irritable man, followed him every moment of the day, questioning decisions, countermanding orders, alienating the help—blaming Lloyd for every difficulty, taking full credit for every accomplishment. His favorite gambit was to taste a dish after preparation and demand that it be thrown out. They had run through four head chefs in six months.

Harry Danton was at the bar. He carried his drink over to a table. Lloyd offered him a cigarette out of the case and said, "Recognize this?"

Danton took it, looked at it and handed it back. "I told a friend to pick out something. Hell, that hasn't got much flash. You don't look so good, Wescott."

"This isn't the best deal in the world."

"Sewed up for next summer?"

"They want me back up there."

"We're about ready to go. I took some guys in, but I got the big end so I got the say. For the land and the house we can go to five. Five million. It'll be a corporation. I talked to a couple of clowns want the job, but I'm not high on them. It's open if you want it."

Lloyd thought for a long time. "Wait right here."

He found the owner in the dining room criticizing the way the waiters were folding the luncheon napkins. Lloyd went up to him. "Mr. Dockerty, am I the manager here?"

Dockerty peered at him. "Of course, Lloyd!"

"Then I must insist that you stop interfering with the management of this hotel. If you have a complaint, speak to me. Stay out of the kitchens. I'm asking the staff to ignore any orders you may give them from now on." The dining room staff was listening.

Dockerty turned pale and then flushed dark red. "I know more about business methods than you ever will! You can't talk to me this way. I own this hotel, I'm not going to stand by and watch you run it into the ground! I can manage my own hotel!"

"There's no such a thing as two managers."

"Then get out! Draw your pay and get out! Come on and I'll make out the check right now. I want you packed and out of here in fifteen minutes. I won't stand for insolence, Wescott."

With the check in his pocket, Lloyd went back to the men's bar and sat down at the table. "Hello, boss," he said.

Danton nodded. He took out a packet of bills in a jeweled clip, separated five hundreds and one five-hundred and handed them to Lloyd. "Go on out and look around. Send a temporary address to the address on this card and they'll mail you the poop to fill out to get on the payroll."

He drove out. He took a long look at the Reno area, and a longer look at Vegas. He saw the blight that over-expansion had brought to Vegas, and winced at the land prices. He checked roads, airlines, trains. And found the town of Oasis Springs, and found the place for the hotel and found out who owned it and found out what they could get it for. Harry Danton stared unbelievingly and said, "But this is nothing! This is from nowhere kid! Chrissake, who'll ever find it when we put it up?"

Lloyd counted the facts on his fingers. "A main highway. Rail, plane and bus transportation. Decent shops in town. Cheap land. Unlimited water supply. Probably a tax break from the county. Let them come to us, Harry."

"But, my God, I'd go nuts in this town in twenty minutes, kid!"

"Harry?"

He sighed. "Okay, okay, okay. It's your baby." Then he looked directly at Lloyd and said, very softly and dangerously, "But I think you better be right, kid."

The Hotel Green Oasis opened on schedule on Saturday, the sixteenth day of January, 1965. Despite fabulously expensive shipments of sod, there was a raw look to the grounds. Yet the hotel itself was enough to take the eye from the raw earth. It had none of the staccato flash of Collins Avenue or Vegas. It was hushed and tasteful, yet still dramatic. Guests, reacting to the special atmosphere, felt more handsome, more witty, more assured. Lloyd had remembered every bad service layout he had ever seen or heard about, and made certain not one of them existed in this hotel. By maximum use of automatic devices and intercom systems, the service was geared to a routine so sleek, so unobtrusive, that even during the first few days there were no major foulups.

The architects who planned the hotel had nothing to do with the Copper Casino. Lloyd supervised the food and liquor setup over there, and Charlie Bliss handled the rest. It was a gaudy horror, full of the fever-flush of money, as perfectly suited to the job as a cash register.

During the opening week the hotel was packed with free loaders from Hollywood, television, the sports world and the newspaper columns. Through Danton's connections, the names were big. The opening splash made it the place to go. From then on a satirical, foul-mouthed little man named Hoppy Hopper kept the publicity wheels turning. He lived in a furnished room in the village because he hated hotels.

Lloyd knew they were over the hump when the house stayed full in the dead season, and when nearby pieces of land were purchased for other hotels and ground was broken. In the summer the county enlarged the airport, and Oasis Springs began to get better scheduled service. New shops opened in the village. Harry Danton flew out often. Finally he decided to make it his headquarters. He wanted two suites, one for living quarters and one for office space. Lloyd objected violently. They made him run the accommodations, food and liquor at the breakeven point. The whole hotel was a shill. The casino was the cream. He couldn't afford to lose two of the best suites. With a crash priority, a separate structure was put up for Harry. It blended with the lines and colors of the hotel. Two bedrooms, two baths, living room, kitchen, large office, air conditioning, small outdoor pool, screen of shubbery. He brought three of his people from Detroit, a woman and two men. They kept apart from the hotel staff, and lived in the village.

Harry said, "You know a funny thing? This is the first damn time in my life I've ever had a house to live in. I think I like it."

In October Lloyd was able to raise his head and look around and see that he had built a good thing, and that from here on in the running of it would get easier. Good lieutenants, after much shifting around, had been broken in. Now there could be some time off. He bought a new car.

Danton went on a trip. Tulsa, in tones of wonder, told Lloyd he had heard Harry had gotten married. Tulsa and Benny both tried to laugh at such ridiculous news, but it was hollow laughter. "Maybe," Lloyd said, "he liked living in a house well enough to put a wife in it. Who is the lucky, lucky girl?"

"Sylvia Kennedy. She used to sing under that name. You remember, Tuls?"

"Sure. That was after Frenchy took her out to the coast and he had a piece of that band that time."

"Say!" Benny said, "Dint Frenchy marry her?"

"Some say yes and some say no, and it didn't make a damn bit of difference to her on account of when he sort of got pushed out that window that time, he didn't even have a pot left. Where'd she go after that, Benny? You know?"

"I heard last year she was back in New York with Big Windy and singing in some little club like. Then they canceled out Big Windy's citizenship. Jeez, Tuls. I don't get it. Sure, people get married, but why marry Sylvia? And having Harry marry her!"

Tulsa reproved Benny heavily. "Shut up and look at it this way. Maybe Harry figures he wants to get married. So what's wrong with Sylvia? She's good-looking. She never did time. You can't count that time they held her four months in L. A. County. That was for questioning, no charges. And she didn't widen an inch. So you can trust her, see? Harry can talk over business and it's okay. And there's a lot of mutual friends, see?"

"I wouldn't marry her," Benny said stubbornly.

"And what pig would marry you?" Tulsa asked, deeply disgusted.

When Harry phoned over and asked him to come over and meet the wife, Lloyd had a preconceived idea of just what she would be like. A brass-haired blonde going to seed, with the gutter voice of the blues shouter. He could remember Miss West in Maine, and he had seen several of Danton's other women.

Harry met him at the door. He was beaming and he had a glass in his hand. "Surprise you, kid? Suprised me too. Never thought I'd take the step. Come on and meet the bride. She's out by the pool. We got in late. We just got up a little while back."

Sylvia sat by the pool in a chair of tubular aluminum and plastic webbing, reading. She wore crisp white shorts and a white halter. She was a long-bodied girl, medium tall, narrow of waist, sleek of leg. Her black hair was of a soft texture and it was pulled back into a bun.

"Honey, this is the guy I was telling you about. Lloyd Wescott. Meet Sylvia, Lloyd."

She put the book aside, looked up at him and smiled and held her hand out to him. Her eyes were a deep brown, almost black, her face well-cut and delicate, her smile warm and personal. "I certainly have heard a great deal about you, Lloyd. Harry has told me a dozen times how pleased he is with what you've done here. I can't wait to take the grand tour." Her voice was low, well-modulated, her diction precise.

"This is the best taste Harry has ever shown," Lloyd said.

"Thank you, sir."

"Why don't you show her around, Lloyd? I got some catching up to do."

"Should I change?" she asked.

"For this time of day, you're practically overdressed, Mrs. Danton."

"Sylvia—please," she said.

He showed her the entire layout, from sun deck to sub-basement. It was a tour he had given others, but he enjoyed it more this time. She had a lithe and pleasing walk, and her questions were intelligent. When they came across Tulsa and Benny she seemed pleased to see them. They seemed almost formal in their attitude toward her.

"That's it," he said when they were through. "Now you get a drink on the house. Pick your bar."

"That one where you look sort of down at the pool, I think. The little one. And something tall with rum and fruit in it."

On the way they passed a bank of slots, half of them in use. She held out her hand and said gravely, "A two bits for a gambling lady?" She pulled the lever, caught three bells, and twenty quarters came tumbling down. "Just call me lady luck," she said with a hint of bitterness. "Say, these things *do* have a pocket. Ten for you and ten for me."

"No."

"I can get terribly cross. Here. Do you gamble at all?"

"Sometimes as much as ten whole dollars a week." They sat on bar stools. She ordered her drink.

As she sipped it she looked at his glass. "Is that just plain ginger ale?"

"While on duty, Sylvia."

"You are a good guide, Lloyd. I might even be able to find my way out of here. Did it shock you to hear Harry got married?"

He watched her face. "Tulsa, Benny and I shared the news. We were all very intrigued."

There was a sudden look of hardness around her eyes. "I see. A lot of jolly speculation going on. Get a complete briefing on me, did you?"

"Some scattered facts."

"How do I shape up, little boy scout?"

"For some reason I can't understand, all of a sudden you want to make me angry. I'm not angry. And if I was, I'd hide it so well you couldn't see it, Mrs. Danton. I know Harry's usual taste. Give him his head and he'd put diamonds in his front teeth. You aren't what I expected. I'm agreeably surprised. And I'm glad for Harry's sake."

"We're both snobs, Lloyd. You see, once upon a time I was exactly what you expected."

"It doesn't seem possible."

"I don't know why I should tell you any personal history. Maybe it's because I may need a friend at court some time. You look bright and talk bright and could possibly be bright. I couldn't say yet."

"I'm bright, Sylvia. And I work at it."

"So take Sylvia at fourteen. She looked eighteen. A kid from Hell's Kitchen. A tough bastard of a kid with a whore mother and an unknown father. She was tough through and through and you don't lose that kind of toughness, my friend. Buy me another of these. She knew every filthy trick in the books and got picked up helping the other kids roll a lush, and got sent to one of those schools and got out by knocking out a matron with a Coke bottle. That was twelve years ago, Lloyd. How am I doing?"

He was shocked by the whispered vehemence of her words. "You've come a long way."

"Before I was fifteen I was traveling with a syndicate car thief named Joey Tower. He got hot so they transferred him to the west coast and I went along. My hair was bleached white. I wore sweaters two sizes too small. I talked with a whine and the language would make a truckdriver shiver. But Joey's boss saw something in the slut, and cut Joey out, with a little help from the slut, who was a very greedy child, and still is."

"Sylvia, I—"

"You started the needle job, and you're going to listen. Joey's boss made some minor improvements, but it was the next guy up the ladder who used his head. He had the docks in S. F. He had a little education. I got on his nerves. He took me to a school. The Demming School, for young ladies. Miss Helen Demming. One look at me and she nearly dropped her teeth. That school was a hundred years old, nearly, and they'd never seen anything like Sylvia. I waited and he was in the office with her a long time and I was accepted, and booked for special tutoring on the side. I was nearly sixteen when he enrolled me. He'd take me out for the weekends. That used to shatter Miss Helen, but she didn't have the nerve to yell cop. At first I wanted to take the place apart, and made a good start at it, but I was just barely smart enough to see what might happen. After six months Lennie wanted to take me out of there, but I kicked up such a storm he gave up. I stuck with it three years, Lloyd. And when I got out, I could walk into any place in the world and be mistaken for a lady. I knew how to dress, and I knew good grooming and good taste. I'd acquired a liking for good literature and good conversation. No matter how much silver at any place setting, they couldn't confuse me. So I took three hundred out of Lennie's wallet one night and went back to New York to meet a nice square, a rich young man of family. When I was down to less than five dollars, I looked up some old contacts. Am I boring you, boy scout?"

"No. Keep going."

"The word was out that wherever I showed, Lennie wanted the favor of having somebody work me over, with special attention to the face. He wanted to present some plastic surgeon with a real problem. You see, there was never any more than one ladder for me, the only ladder I could climb. I went back and got on my own ladder. Before they could work me over, I said I wanted to deal. I said I had some dope about Lennie. I did. He had a grift on the side that wasn't going into the pot and was pulling a bill a day. I wasn't going to open up until my face came into it. A little big shot tried to get it all, but I'd only hint until I got passed all the way up to Frenchy. I gave it to him. He sent a specialist out and he checked and then he sent another kind of specialist and so now Lennie is somewhere halfway to Alcatraz with half a hardware store wired to him. By then Frenchy had married me. I think the education stoned him. I had a convertible and a duplex and a mink and a hatful of jewelry, but I also had Frenchy. He gripped a fork with his fist, and when he ate it sounded like buffalo stampeding through a swamp. But he was a sharp dresser. Class with a K. Shoulders out to here. When they moved him to the coast, he decided I could sing. Much to everybody's astonishment, I nearly could. The voice is true, but the range is narrow and it's weak. Don't look so nervous. I won't do any singing in your hotel, thank you."

"Am I looking nervous?"

"I'm on a talking jag on two drinks. Please order me another, noble boy scout. Frenchy was transferred to the coast. I've told you that. Where was I? Oh, yes. He had decided I was bright, and he asked my advice on little business problems. I buttered him good. He was about three grades down from the top, but I got him thinking he was the top. So they started to squeeze him. He fought back. They said they wanted to mediate. A meeting was fixed. In a high building. Frenchy forgot to wear his parachute. There was a stink. Grand jury investigation. Little congressmen pattering and panting about. They held me and asked me nine billion questions, and nine billion times I looked blank and said, 'I don't know. My husband never talked to me about business. I thought he was in investments.' It didn't work very well, because they could tie me to Lennie.

"When they gave up I drove my convertible back to New York and reported into Windsalla, one more step up the ladder. I was a public figure, and I hadn't talked. Windsalla approved on both counts. It was a fat year until they moved in on him and returned him to Mother Italia. He wanted me to come with him. Not Sylvia. The parting gift lasted two months. Next the mink. Then the jewelry started going. Through connections I got into some clubs, but I couldn't last. Two weeks ago I was singing in a very sour little club in the east fifties, holding my own only because I had some very blue material. I was billed as the ex-darling of mobland. And I felt very ex indeed. Harry saw the billing and came in. We've known each other for years. Afterwards I went to his hotel. We both got off on a crying jag. Old times and old faces. It seemed a very solemn and wonderful idea to get married. By morning he still meant it. At the end of the waiting period, he still meant it. So here is Sylvia, back in the big feather bed after a cold bad time."

"A hard gal, through and through."

"Right down to bed rock, Lloyd. I've got a heart like a stone."

"Poor defeated woman. My addition says you're all

of twenty-six. Close to the end of your life. Slippers and rocking chair for you, Sylvia."

"Do tell me the exciting story of your life?"

"Do you go for drama, conflict, tension?"

"Oh, very much!"

"Here it is. I was born twenty-nine years ago, the younger of two boys, in Royalsville, a thriving city of six thousand in eastern Ohio, near Youngstown. I attended the public schools there, starring in basketball, track and baseball. My father was a druggist. At the time of his retirement he owned three stores. My parents now live in Bradenton, Florida, in what is advertised as the largest trailer court in the world. My brother is married and has four children and operates a mill and lumber yard in Portland, Oregon. I attended a famed school of hotel administration, and was kept out of a couple of wars because of some healed spots on my right lung from a touch of tuberculosis I never knew I had. Upon graduation I worked for a large hotel chain, then got out to become an assistant manager of an independent. I'm a pretty good hotel man, and I've had breaks. I'm damn young for this job, and damn well paid. I save money. I exercise regularly. All my vices are moderate. My relatives all think I am in a wacky profession and they keep hinting I ought to get married. I came close once, but she was all the time smelling of spearmint, a flavor I can't abide. She married an associate professor of philology, and my spies inform me that she weighs a bouncing hundred and ninety. I hope my story hasn't been too gripping."

He smiled at her but the smile faded when he saw she was looking very solemn, almost sad. She had that shine in her eyes that indicates tears are close. "You know, you did that well. You did just what I deserve. I think you did just what I needed, Lloyd."

"What do you need?"

"I need to stop feeling so damn sorry for myself all the time. I've felt that way for years. I wanted to shock you. I wanted you to come up with a lot of asinine questions. But you put me very neatly in my place. I thought I was being dramatic. I guess I was being silly."

"Just a little bit silly. Not enough to count."

"All I ever really wanted was a guy with one drug store who could maybe build it up to three. You're going to be good for me, Lloyd. You have . . . balance."

"And you are the young wife of a man who owns the major piece of a very thriving hotel managed with imagination and integrity by a sterling young man who, back in the days of the tap center in basketball, was known fondly as Leaping Lloyd. So just be a young wife. Now you've gone legit. Now you're as square as the rest of us."

"All right," she said. "Young housewife. Shake, fellow square."

"Walk you back?"

"You run along and manage the hell out of this place. I'm going to have this kind man mix up another of these juicy things."

5

The naked bearded man lay in the sheltered space between brown rocks and thought of all the people he had been, of all the curious turns and twists of the road that had finally brought him to this place. Had it started when Danton came to Maine? Or when Dockerty had fired him? Or had it really started that first day with Sylvia when, for no reason that either of them could isolate later, they had reached very quickly a level of utter frankness.

He knew when the other phase of it had started. After that first day he did not see her for a week, but he thought about her a great deal. She was in his mind more often than was reasonable or understandable. The thought of her married to Harry made him feel slightly queasy, yet there was no reason, he thought, to feel that way. She was certainly far from a virgin bride, probably as far as you could get.

There was that Joey Tower and then somebody she didn't name, and then Lennie and Frenchy and Windsalla. And God knows how many in between, or, earlier, how many sordid episodes in the alleys and hallways and staircases and packing boxes and parked cars of Hell's Kitchen. She was certainly too hardened to feel squeamish about Harry's flabby fifty-three-year-old body, or the hard round pot on the front of him. No matter how much polish had been added, this was still a cheap tramp, a consort of criminals, a hardened chippy, who had wearily, drunkenly, endured all imaginable orgy and debauch. And yet . . .

Harry asked him to stop over at his place one evening and have a drink with them. One of Harry's other business partners was there, a man who had no piece of the hotel, but operated a trucking line in the Texas, Louisiana, Mississippi area, a man named Guntry with a long red wrinkled face and neck, a harsh high-pitched voice, and three fingers of his left hand missing. Sylvia wore a very plain yellow cotton dress. She seemed sullen and remote. Her conversation, though polite, was limited. Guntry had no small talk. All he wanted to talk was tractors and trailers and cost per mile of operation and expansion to Pensacola and how much it would cost.

Guntry wanted to write down some figures, so he and Harry moved to the far corner of the big living room. Sylvia sat on a chaise longue, ankles crossed, both hands holding her drink, looking down into it.

"You're not a bundle of cheer tonight," Lloyd said.

"I'm sorry. I don't think I can whip up a nervous giggle."

"Anything wrong?"

"Nothing special. It was just an extremely short honeymoon."

When Harry spoke to her there was a nasty-sweet edge to his voice that Lloyd found embarrassing. He left as soon as he could. The next day, in town, he saw Sylvia's car, the baby blue MG Harry had bought her. He had been about to return to the hotel. Instead he walked around until he spotted her coming out of a dress shop, a package in her arm.

"Coke, lady?"

"Lloyd! You startled me. This is more a beer type day, isn't it."

"That there place over there lady has got draft beer and yuh git to set on a saddle at the bar, by Godfrey."

She inspected the saddles and settled for a booth near the back. They got huge mugs of dark beer. "I was grim last night, I guess."

"Sort of."

"I can talk to you, Lloyd. I can talk to that nice boy scout face of yours. Your good deed is just to listen. I jumped at this marriage, Lloyd. God, how I jumped. And I made it damn well clear to him it wasn't love. He said he'd never been convinced there was any such thing anyway. So now he wants love. I've got to go all dewy when he's around. Mist right up. Gasp and bleat and whinny. He is the sort of human being who has to have everything, every last atom and molecule of everything he touches. He gets sore when I do what he calls 'hiding in a damn book.' He tells me I'm cold. If I stop telling him what a great man he is, then I'm being critical. Damn it all, I was willing to marry him, but I don't want my privacy invaded." She laughed suddenly. "That sounds wild, doesn't it?"

"Is he in love do you think?"

"With me? No. He just wants to whomp the spirit out of me. He wanted me out here. Marriage was my price. I said I was getting too old for coeducational vacations. I also said that if you do too much of that sort of thing, the vacations get shorter and shorter until finally when you're forty they only last twenty minutes in some crib in Trinidad. It was my price and he paid it, and now I think he figures I've got some paying to do. I can do a lot of pretending, but it gets pretty wearing. Lennie had a bull pup once. It liked to grab one end of a towel and have you yank him around on the other end. Every chance he'd get, he'd snatch a little more towel until finally there wasn't any room for your fingers. Harry is like that."

"He's left me alone."

"Try to leave and see."

He stared at her. "I could give notice and leave. Why not?"

"You could be desk clerk in a flea bag. You'll never get a good job managing a good hotel. Not for long. Not in this country. And I know just how he'd fix you. Through the unions. Hiring you would be a guarantee of a walkout on some other pretext. Harry never lets people go. He likes them to try it, though, because he likes to have them crawl back."

"He's no monster!"

"Of course not. In his business there are certain rules. He's carried those rules over from the rackets to the legit enterprises. Nobody leaves. No top people. You're in for life. But don't kick about it. You have it good. I've seen the bonus list. You're down for five thousand."

"I still don't like it."

"Cheer up, Lloyd. You'll be as bad as I was last night."

When he had the chance he checked her theory with Harry one day when they were alone in Lloyd's office.

"This is running smooth now, Harry. Maybe it will eventually get so smooth I'll get bored and go find somebody else who wants a hotel managed."

Harry grinned. "Don't get bored then."

"Seriously, suppose I did want to take off some day?"

"You'd get an argument."

"But I could go, couldn't I?"

"What is this, kid? What's chewing you? You need a raise? You unhappy or something? If you're getting the job licked, drift with it. You want to work too hard all your life?"

"Sometimes you get so you need a change."

"When you need a change, let me know. I'll send you to look over hotel problems in Paris. That's a legitimate deduction. If you don't like Paris, they got hotels everywhere. If you're restless, we can send a secretary along with you. I got a contact who can come up with a real class kid, college level."

"What you're saying is, I work for you from here on in."

Harry stood up. "Is that so bad? Am I some clown? Isn't the pay right? Listen, I'll tell you something. In every business they got key personnel, right? Okay, you're key personnel. In a lot of businesses they got a turnover problem with key personnel. G. E. has it. General Motors has it. Even the Air Force has it. But you know what ratio of turnover I run on key personnel? None. No ratio at all. I don't want you trying to spoil my record, kid. If right now you got an itch, that's okay. It's letdown. You've worked like a dog. Tell you what you do. Draw a thousand and take off for a week. The house won't fall down. Go away someplace. Go get laid."

"Thanks, Harry. I'm not that restless. I was just thinking."

"Don't think too much."

"Suppose I goofed on the job. Would I get fired?"

"If you goof, I lose money. If I lose money, my partners lose money. If they lose money, they say, 'What the hell, Harry! What are you doing to us?' Then I say, 'Look, boys. This Wescott goofed off. He dogged it on purpose.' Then they say, 'So what did you do to him?' Much as I like you, kid, I can't let my partners down. They put money in it. So then I have to have proof, see? Or maybe they'll think I was screwing them to buy them out cheap or something. Maybe the proof is something out of the paper. Manager of the Hotel Green Oasis dead in car smash or drowns in Lake Tahoe or shoots self or something."

The whole length of Lloyd's spine felt cold. "Are you trying to scare me, Harry?"

"Hell, no, I'm not trying to scare you. I'm telling you. I'd be in a hell of a position and, much as I like you, I'd have to do something about it, wouldn't I? I can't start going soft. You start going soft and they run in from all sides like a pack of dogs and chew the legs right out from under you. Friendship is friendship, but number one is number one, Lloyd. I'd be helpless in such a situation. There's only one way to go and that's get a sickness so bad you can't work any more. If a bad thing like that happens, you'd stay right on the payroll long as you live. Hell, if I tried to welsh on that, my partners would raise hell with me. They know when you got to do the right thing by a right guy, just the same as you got to put all the clamps on a wrongo."

After Harry had left the office Lloyd sat quite still for a long time marveling over what he had just heard. Do your job or be killed. It was incredible, impossible—and perfectly true. The Dantons had brought into legitimate business the code of the gang. He shuddered and went back to work.

Aside from Sylvia, there was no one he could talk to about this situation in which he found himself. He had hired his own staff. Charlie Bliss was at his own executive level. It was inconceivable that he could talk to Charlie. Charlie had a head and a face like a polished white stone, a stone you pick up in a stream bed and turn it this way and that way and decided it does resemble a man's head and face. See, these things here are the eyes and that is the mouth.

Hoppy Hopper was no confidant. His relationship with Hopper was not good. Some of Hopper's publicity ideas had not been in keeping with the decor Lloyd was trying to establish. Hopper seemed to feel that the hotel would be best served if all news services people could watch the debut of some exceptionally bosomy Italian singer in the Caravan Room wearing a cellophane dress while, simultaneously, two important Trendex comedians were bashing each other's noses in the men's room. Lloyd had complained until Harry had ordered Hoppy to check out new ideas with Lloyd for approval. This Hoppy did with the worst possible grace.

Lloyd realized that there was no one he could turn to. He had not thought of himself as a loner. He had many good friends. Yet essentially he had moved in his own way, in his own pattern.

In December Sylvia began to spend more time in the hotel. He would find her in one of the bars, or out by the big pool. Each time he saw her he went to her and spoke to her for a time. She seemed tense and unhappy, her eyes shadowed by fatigue. When Harry went off on a business trip, saying he wouldn't return until after the first of the year, Lloyd felt a sense of elation that he could not pin down until he realized that he felt he could talk to Sylvia with less strain.

Harry left on a Friday. On Sunday, realizing he hadn't seen Sylvia for three days, he began an aimless stroll around the grounds that inevitably took him to her door. He could see her through the screen, sitting alone, in profile against the bright sunlight that came in from the pool.

When he spoke she got up and came to the door, pushed it open and said, "Come in."

As soon as he could see her clearly, his jaw dropped. Her left eye was ludicrous. It was deep blue and purple and indigo, fading into plum and saffron that stained half the left side of her face. It had a humid bulging look. It was slitted and, from far back, a thin slice of dark brown eye looked gravely out at him.

"What happened?"

"Let me see now. I ran into a door. Yes, I ran into a door." She turned away from him suddenly, white pleated skirt swirling.

He followed her and said, "What *did* happen?"

"Skip it, Lloyd. Call it a parting gift. Something to remember him by."

"Why should he do a thing like that?"

She turned and faced him. They were standing by the glass doors that opened onto the pool area. She smiled at him. "Poor boy scout. Full of outrage. Sore because he marked me. Usually he's much more considerate. Sometimes I have to wear long sleeves, and sometimes I have to pick a sun suit without a bare midriff, but those are just little problems any girl can handle."

"Does he do this often?"

"It's getting oftener. I don't conform so good. It's a

very standard way of breaking somebody down to a manageable size. It hurts, so you try to avoid being hurt, and pretty soon you're following orders like a nice little lamb. My God, don't look at me with those sheep eyes, Lloyd. I'm an expert on eyes. In three more days dark glasses will hide it. This is mild. Joey Tower used to bounce me off the walls. It gave him his kicks. But I was a kid then. And I . . . healed easier." The hard voice faltered.

"Sylvia!"

"I don't want sympathy or understanding. This was just a little marital quarrel. It's none of your business. I've never had to lean on anybody in my whole life. I'm not going soft at this late date. You're just a . . ." And her voice broke completely, mouth twisting and trembling like a child fighting tears. He took her wrists and she came reluctantly into his arms. He held her and her tears came. He moved back away from the glass doors, still holding her through all the lost and lonely paroxysms, the wrenching sobs, the slow fading of tears, back to a time of deep breathing with a small catch at the end of each breath. She turned away from him quickly and left the room. His shirt and the lapel of his white jacket were damp, and there was a smudge of her lipstick. It was ten minutes before she came out, quite shyly.

"I'm a damn fool. Thanks, Lloyd. I can't even remember the last time I cried for real. I've faked enough times, but it isn't the same."

"Glad to be of service. But I've accumulated some incriminating evidence. There is one thing about a big hotel, Sylvia, that perhaps you don't know. The spy system is practically perfect. When staff duties are routine, there's nothing to do but watch the guests and the other staff people. If one bellhop spends thirty minutes in a room with a bored female guest, before the next hour is up the second pastry chef knows the woman's choice in perfume and underwear because somehow that data filters down from the room maid."

"I've got something that will take that out," she said. She came back with a small bottle.

"Shall I take it off?"

"No need. Turn toward the light, please."

She scrubbed industriously, biting her lower lip. She recapped the bottle, surveyed her work. "There. Gone."

He put his hands on her shoulders. She looked at him, slightly startled. "Lloyd, don't—"

With his lips on hers she said "Don't" one more time, and then surrendered. From a place far away he heard the bottle drop to the floor. It was as though they had kissed a thousand times. It was a perfect fit of contour, contour of body, of emotion and of need. They parted, gasping, dizzied and appalled. She steadied herself, gave him the cloth she had used on the coat. "Wipe your mouth. I'll be damned if I'm going to get all mixed up in a . . . This is the craziest thing anybody could possibly . . . I'm not going to let you be the little dog on the railroad tracks, Lloyd. Because it can't mean that much. I can't mean that much in that kind of way to anybody. I'm just a . . ."

And with a sound quite like a sob she came back into his arms.

His feeling of apprehension did not come until later, until the sun was lower, until they lay dreamy, languorous and sated, sharing a single cigarette. He tried to push the cold knowledge of danger out of his mind, the awareness that this was an incident of monumental foolishness. It had always been his practice to avoid any emotional relationship with a guest. There had always been ample opportunity to be a fool. He had slipped once, on his first hotel job. A merciful manager had put the fear of God into him, explaining in detail exactly what could happen to his career.

The implications of this were far worse. This was the wife of the owner. It did not matter that she was lonely, unhappy, abused and beautiful. It did not matter that she was passionately demanding and shatteringly exciting. This was Harry's wife.

He began to dress hurriedly. She left the room, carrying her clothing, moving quick and tall and gracefully. She came back wearing the plain yellow dress he had seen before.

"Don't go for a minute," she said. "We have to talk."

They were both sobered, both apprehensive. This was a way to commit suicide. They told each other with deliberate emphasis that this was an unfortunate incident, and the sane, adult thing to do was to forget it ever happened, and certainly never let it happen again. Yes, it was just one of those things. If they tried, they could easily get back into their previous relationship. Perhaps even that relationship was too friendly. They told each other these things as though they were arguing on the same side against a third party. And, as the sweeping statements began to lose emphasis, they both began to realize they were whistling into the wind. And they stopped talking.

"What you said about hotels," she said.

"Yes?"

"We'll have to be *so* careful, Lloyd. So terribly careful."

"I know."

"And we'll have to keep our heads. We can't ever get overconfident, and careless."

He was very alert during the next few days for any change in attitude toward him on the part of the staff. He knew that if there was talk, if he had been seen going to Harry's place and staying there for two hours on a Sunday afternoon while Sylvia was alone, he would surprise a look of speculation, see whisperings.

One thing favored the intrigue. He had never maintained a regular work routine. He inspected every segment of the operations at least once a day, but at unexpected times. And he covered the ground twice or three times often enough in one day so that one visit was no guarantee that he might not stop again. It made for a taut house. But there was one serious handicap to the intrigue. He had made it a practice to keep his secretary informed of his whereabouts at all times, so he could be reached at once in case of an emergency. This had to be altered. He did it gradually, and when finally she complained, he told her that things were now running so smoothly that the old routine could be relaxed. He was with Sylvia twice more before Harry returned, once at dawn on a Tuesday, once at midnight a few days later. Each episode was as carefully planned and timed as a military operation.

After Harry came back it was impossible. It sickened him to think of Harry with her. One day she slipped him a note saying she would be at that place in the village, the beer place, at three in the afternoon. She was in the back booth when he came in. Her smile was brilliant.

"What's up?"

"I just wanted to see you, Lloyd, and talk. I wanted to tell you things are easier for me. I can handle the marriage better now. I'm not as vulnerable as I was. I'm not so alone."

"Does he seem to have any kind of suspicion?"

"Oh, no. None at all. Anyway, he's too damn busy being sore at Charlie Bliss."

"What about?"

"More state people smelling around. Charlie got too hungry during the holidays. I heard him give Charlie his orders. No more grift for six months. So Charlie has to operate on the legal house percentage no matter how big a mark comes in. He looked as though someone had run over his dog."

He stared at her. "I don't think I understand."

She stared back. "My God, you poor dunce! I thought you knew."

"Knew what?"

"Darling, this is the flossiest clip joint in the world. Did you think for one minute Harry and his partners would settle for the legal house take all the way down the line? There's nothing rough about it. The little people with two or three hundred to bet get the same break here they'll get anywhere in Nevada. But once in a while they'll get a mark. Remember those two men from Houston in the middle of December? They dropped a hundred and eighty thousand."

Lloyd remembered them. "They were cheated?"

"They sure as hell were."

"How is it possible? There are inspections. The books are open. If the casino nets too much, can't they close it down and take the equipment apart?"

"First item. There are three sets of books. Three, because Harry is giving the partners just enough to keep them quiet. Second item. Charlie Bliss is the greatest mechanic in the business, and some of his men are almost as good as he is. This is the electronic age. Some of Charlie's gimmicks will fit in the palm of your hand. Readily detachable. No heavy wiring. No crude stuff like in Havana at the Tropicana and the National Casino. This is a slick operation. The casino will stand a complete inspection at any time. But you won't find any big smart money gambled here. The word is out."

"Couldn't they have gotten enough money off those men from Houston anyway?"

"No, my innocent lamb. They might have dropped fifteen or twenty thousand and quit. With a gimmicked game, if the control is perfect, and Charlie's always is, you can use psychology. They lost it on the wheel. Charlie saw they were using a system, a doubling system on red and black. So he let their system work. He let them win thirty thousand and then eased them back down to even, and then let them come up to thirty-five and pushed them back down again, and then let them come up to fifty. That was nearly a mistake, because one wanted to quit then and they nearly did. After he pushed them up and down about eight times, they got the idea he wanted them to get. They doubled their opening stake, figuring the system was working and they could get up to maybe a hundred thousand by playing twice as heavy. He had them then. He let them get up to sixty thousand and by then neither of them had any desire to quit. They'd been drinking and playing the wheel for five hours. They were ripe and he dropped the boom on them. They were on black then. So he hit the red three times, then the zero, then the red four times, then the double zero, and then three more reds. That put them ninety thousand down and they were pretty sick. Charlie stopped the wheel to give them a chance to write checks. They put ninety thousand on the black, so Charlie fed them another double zero. Those were two sick Texans. Thirteen spins and no black. One character playing the double zero with twenty dollar chips got very healthy, picking up all of fourteen hundred bucks."

Up until then Lloyd had taken pride in the hotel, pride in what he had done. He had not thought much about the gambling or the casino. It was spoiled for him. He saw that all he had done was built a very superior web, so that Charlie could crouch in a dark corner and wait for the juiciest flies to blunder in. Clip joint. A very superior clip joint, but that did not matter.

He told himself that it was none of his business. His job was to run a renowned hotel and run it as well as he could. But the taste was gone. What good did it do to fight for Triple A beef to feed the innocent about to be trimmed? It did not help to know that Charlie had shelved his toys for six months. Six months would end and there would be another mark to be taken, more false entries to be made. He knew he did not care any more, yet he forced himself to be diligent.

When Harry took a trip in February he was with Sylvia again. She seemed the only desirable thing in a tasteless world. Their hunger for each other was great, and hunger bred daydreams. "Darling," she said softly, lips close to his throat, "we don't belong here. We'll go to some place where no one can ever find us."

His disgust with his job was like a sickness. He had become more irritable with the staff. They responded by becoming slightly slack in their work. Only an expert could have seen the tiny changes. A smear of grease on the stainless hood over the main range. A spot on linen. A noisy bushing in an electric motor.

"Some place far away," he said. "An island in the south seas. Swim in the surf. Live on cocoanuts."

It was Sylvia who said, quite casually, "Of course we could manage it if we took off with enough money, enough of Harry's lovely money."

They were sitting then, on opposite sides of a small table. Her words seemed to hang in the air for a long time. They looked at each other and looked uneasily away. Her laugh was nervous. "That is an idea we'd better drop," she said. "And fast."

But the idea stayed with him, and grew. It was stolen money. What harm to take it from a thief. He found many pretexts to go to the Copper Casino. It was completely staffed by Charlie's people, with the exception of the food handlers and bartenders. Lloyd soon saw that he would have no more chance of acquiring any of that money than would an outsider. Charlie had thought of every possible protection against a stickup.

Yet the idea persisted. When he finally saw how he could take money, it was ridiculously simple. Winners felt uneasy about having cash on their persons, or in their rooms. They put it in the hotel safe, a stout modern box in the office behind the reservation desk. As he put a thick envelope away one evening, he wondered why he had not thought of the guests' money. The head cashier, Mrs. Boyer, had one key to the safe and he had the other. They were the only two keys, and they had to be used simultaneously. Harry had a complete set of two keys locked away somewhere. When Mrs. Boyer went off duty, she turned her key over to Harmon, or whatever other person was on night desk duty. Lloyd never let his key out of his possession. It was a nuisance to have to come down to use the key, but it seemed safer. When the safe was unlocked, the door hung open. It was designed that way as a precaution against leaving it accidentally unlocked. He had heard of taking an imprint of a key and getting another made, but he did not know how to go about getting such an imprint, or where to go to get a key made. When he was with Mrs. Boyer, she would hand her key over and he would work both of them, give hers back to her. When the house was full and play was heavy, there was often a good deal of money in the safe. He tried to think of the easiest way to manage it. It would not take a great deal of tension to keep the door closed. If it remained closed it would look as though it were locked.

When, in April, Harry went on a three day visit to Los Angeles, Lloyd explained his idea to Sylvia. She was very nervous about it. They had talked about it enough times so that it was not difficult to talk, and at times the talk seemed academic—it seemed to be talk of something that would never occur.

"Would he contact the police?" he asked. "It isn't his money."

"Never. He wouldn't yell cop. He'd make the losses good. And then he'd send people after us."

"They'd never find us. Not if there's enough money."

"There'll have to be enough. Will your idea work?"

"I think so."

"You'll have to rehearse it. You'll have to actually go through with it once without taking the money."

"I know."

She clung to him. "I'm scared, Lloyd. I'm terribly frightened."

"What else can we do? What else is there in the world for us to do?" he asked, his voice dull.

The rehearsal worked perfectly. When he had a chance to tell her she said she had decided she couldn't go through with it. In May Harry became more brutal with her. And Harry complained to Lloyd about bad service in the hotel. Things were moving toward the inevitable showdown. On the first of May Harry left for two weeks on a business trip to New Orleans, Miami and San Juan. They held each other tightly in the grey of a long dawn and said it would have to happen now. They told each other it was what they had to do. She said she would pack. He packed what he would need. He managed to get their suitcases into the back end of the Pontiac without being observed.

They coordinated it carefully. The best time seemed to be early morning, right after Mrs. Boyer came on. He came down carrying the empty blue canvas bag. He went through into his own office. His own secretary was at work. He said good morning to her, and spent the next five minutes looking over departmental reports. He did not see or understand a figure he looked at.

"Betty."

"Yes, Mr. Wescott."

"I'd like you to go get hold of Tony Arco and check liquor stores against this inventory list. Don't bother with back bar stock. Just the cases. It shouldn't take over an hour."

When she had gone, he took a deep breath. He took an envelope out of his desk drawer, went out into the other office where Mrs. Boyer worked alone and said, "Let me take your key, please."

As usual, she handed him the whole key ring, first separating the safe key from the group. He went to the safe. His back was to her. He opened the door, put his envelope inside, and then, as he closed the door, inserted the rubber window wedge he had purchased in the village and shaved down with a razor to the proper thickness. It was out of sight when the door was closed, and made sufficient tension to hold it closed. He made a mock of turning the locks, took her keys back to her. As he handed them to her he said, "I sent Betty off on something that will take at least an hour, Mrs. Boyer." She looked up at him inquiringly, face and expression like that of an aged and truculent pug dog. "Would you do me a favor and go find Foster and give this to him?" This was a report from the heating contractor recommending the installation of another blower in one of the longer airconditioning ducts. Foster, head of maintenance, had been waiting for the report for days.

"Of course, Mr. Wescott," she said, getting out of her chair. "Do you know where he might be. I *know* he won't be in that little office of his."

"Try the roof deck first. There's something wrong with the fountain again."

He knew Foster would be on the roof. That would give him five to seven minutes. He had timed it. As soon as she had gone, he raced into his office, snatched the blue bag, dropped it on the floor beside the safe. He pulled the door open, picked up the wedge when it fell. He scooped out the thick stack of envelopes in the big drawer used for guest valuables. Two big double handfuls filled the blue bag. He zipped it shut, closed the safe door, replacing the wedge, carried the bag into his office and put it out of sight on the floor behind his desk. He was breathing hard. He had worked just inside an open door, not quite in view of the lobby. The two desk men were ten steps away from the open door, and came in often during the day. Two girl cashiers were on the front this time of day, and either of them could have stepped in. The main switchboard was fifteen feet from the open door. It was a calculated risk. When he dropped the bag beside his desk he checked the sweep second hand of his watch and saw that it had taken just forty seconds.

He sat behind his desk and saw Mrs. Boyer return. He went out and asked for her key again. "Sorry. I should have put both of these in at the same time. How is the fountain coming?"

"Between cuss words, I would guess from what he said it will be working before noon."

"Good." He retrieved the rubber wedge and this time he relocked the safe. When he gave her the key, he said, "Tell Betty I've gone into the village on some errands."

Guests who checked valuables were informed they could be retrieved between the hours of nine and eleven, unless they were checking out. Mrs. Boyer said, "Suppose I have to get into the safe, Mr. Wescott?"

"Stall them along," he said, smiling. "I won't be long."

He walked out of the hotel, slowly, trying to look casual. His legs trembled. He got into the car, and as he turned around, he looked once at the hotel, looked at it for the last time, and then drove down the road. The blue MG was parked in the supermarket lot. Sylvia stood waiting in a patch of shade. She walked out and got into the car beside him, yanked the door shut. He drove away.

She looked tautly ahead. Her face looked white and shiny.

"Got it?"

"Yes."

"How much?"

"I have no idea. Enough, though."

"My God, I'm scared. I'm scared. I'm scared."

"Easy, honey. Take deep breaths. Harry is away. This is how it will work. By noon they'll just be annoyed with me. They won't start to get upset until midafternoon. Even then, they won't tie us together. There won't be any panic until tonight, and I don't think they'll get into that safe until tomorrow."

"I think I'll be scared all the rest of my life. You don't know what they're capable of. You don't know what they can do."

"Nothing they can do can be worse than staying there. We'll cross at Juarez some time tomorrow. It's further, but it's safer. We'll push it hard tonight. After we're over, you'll cheer up."

But she hadn't. She had stayed in panic. Her love-making had been conditioned by her tension and her fear. Only after they had gotten to Talascatan did she begin to seem a little more like herself. One hundred and ten thousand dollars seemed like a great deal of money. But when you thought that it was only sixty percent of what Charlie had stolen from the two Texans, it did not seem like so very much. All of her life had been cruel and hard, but it had not killed a tenderness in her, a capacity for love which she denied having. They could make some kind of a life, and try to make it good.

"You," she said, as they walked back in the velvety night from Talascatan to the motel, "You are what I never had and what I wanted and couldn't let myself know I wanted it. A three drugstore man. A man who grew up on shady streets. A man with some boy left in him. We won't make it, Lloyd, if we loaf for the rest of our life. I want to work. I want us to work on something together."

"Like?"

"We'll loaf for a while, then maybe we can start something. A little place where you can eat and have a clean room and a drink. No staff. Just maybe a couple of local servants. Nothing so big anybody will ever hear of it. Just a little place in a hidden corner of the world."

"Kids?"

"We've never talked about that, have we? Remember when I told you not to worry? I didn't tell you why. I guess you should know, and maybe it will be important to you and you will feel cheated, but I couldn't tell you before. I've had two abortions. The first one cost sixty dollars and the place was filthy and I felt fine in a week. The second one cost fifteen hundred and the little sanitarium was immaculate, and it nearly killed me, and it fixed me so there won't be any. Are you terribly sorry?"

"I don't know. I don't think so. I always thought I'd like kids around. If I have to have them around, somebody will be able to spare some kids to the reech Americano."

"You're nice, Lloyd. Now I think we're going to have a long and happy life, and I'm going to try to stop being afraid, really."

"Long and happy," he said, and stopped on the shoulder of the dark road and kissed her, and they went on, hand in hand, swinging their clasped hands. That was the night Tulsa, Benny and Valerez waited. So her life was short indeed, and as unpretty as a short life can be made.

6

His legs began to feel chilled. He sat up and saw that the shadow of one of the western rocks lay across them. He sat up and scratched his beard and stretched until his shoulders creaked. He had been far away, and had thought a long time, and had remembered many things vividly. Perhaps there could never be a single explicit answer to the question of why it had happened. Infatuation, the feeling of being trapped, pity, sexual autohypnosis, perhaps all had conjoined to provide him with a rationalization. It served him at the time, and carried him along through a series of acts he would once have thought impossible even to contemplate.

As he dressed slowly, he thought of what all the people he had known would think of him. Even though Harry wouldn't call in the police, he could not keep it from the staff. The staff would know, and then it would become known throughout the special world of the big resort hotels. "You remember, Wescott? Real tall guy. Good operator. Young. Know what the son of a bitch did? Ran off with the owner's wife and a couple of hundred grand. It was all hushed up. Isn't that a hell of a thing?"

And they would talk about it on the late desk shifts and in the linen rooms and behind the bars. And shrug and say it goes to show you can't ever really figure people out.

There would be talk too, in another world, in a shadowy world of hotel rooms, race tracks, private rooms in road houses, back rooms in bars. They would talk about it from another angle. "You know what happened to Harry? He married that Sylvia, the one that was married to Frenchy. He had this kid running his big new hotel. So the kid takes off with Sylvia and a big chunk of the take. How far did they get? How the hell should I know how far they got? Are you stupid or something? The only thing I know is one thing, pal. The word isn't out. Nobody at all is looking for that pair. So you figure it out your own way."

He walked slowly back to the hut. There would be other people talking, too. His brother and his wife. His parents in the trailer in Bradenton. Sad talk. Speculation. He knew they would go to the police. He could see them talking to the police—or to Harry. And he would see Harry's spread hands, the wide-eyed look of complete innocence. "How the hell should I know where your son went, Mr. Wescott? I was away. I come back and I find he's walked out. I did a hell of a lot for that boy, and he took off without even giving notice. What's that? They traced him as far as the Mexican border? Then maybe you better look down there instead of asking me questions. I'm a busy man."

He thought of his own people and tried to feel sadness and regret. He could, but the emotion was muted. They were far away. They mourned a man who was dead. That was a sad thing and it could not be helped. They could take no pleasure in the man who the son and brother had become. They would not even be able to recognize him. There could be no talk between them, nothing in common. The boy part of the man died in a Mexican motel. The Lloyd Wescott of other years, the efficient, smiling host was like somebody he had once known, and not known very well. They could never understand or condone what this man planned to do. One turned the other cheek. Revenge was barbaric. Murder was unthinkable.

He began to be able to work harder and longer. One high school summer he had worked on a road gang, pick and shovel work. But the hours had been shorter, the breaks more frequent. He had never done manual labor this difficult. The men and boys he worked with seemed tireless. He knew he would never again think of a Mexican as a man dozing, leaning on a wall, sombrero tipped over his eyes. He could not yet do as much as they did, but he could take pride in being harder and stronger and more tireless than ever before in his life. He slept when dark came, and got up in greyness when the chickens were making the first sleepy sounds of awakening. His hands grew hard. He gained weight very slowly. His muscles were like ropes under hide that was nearly as dark as that of anyone in the settlement. He knew that soon he would be able to leave.

Then he became sick. They were working on one of the farthest hillsides, chopping out the tough growth, dragging it into the valley. He worked in a place protected from the wind, stripped to the waist. The cold driving rain came almost without warning, drenching all of them. They found shelter and, after the hour-long rain had passed, began to work again. He felt curiously lightheaded. When they headed for the huts, he knew he was sick. He could not eat. He lay under all the covering they could spare, and he could not get warm. He shivered violently. They gave him remedies. After a time he became so hot he could not stand it under the blankets. Later he slept. When he awakened he knew it was the middle of the night. One of the boys was whining in his sleep. Armando and Concha slept in the other room. Isabella and the boys slept on the pallets in this room. They were rolled up and put out of the way during the daytime. He had never been so cold. His shivering was like a continual shudder, and there was a painful chattering of his broken teeth. He lay fully dressed under the coverings, hugging himself. In spite of the faint red glow of the charcoal, he could see the plume of his breath in the moonlight that came through the smoke hole in the thatch. Others would sleep in coldness this night that he might be warmed.

He lay with his eyes squeezed shut, trying to control the shivering, and gave a start when he felt a light touch on his shoulder. He could make out Isabella on her knees, leaning over him.

"You are very cold," she whispered.

"I am all right."

"No. It is not right." She moved away into the shadows and when she came back he felt her spread more covering over him.

"That is yours. You will freeze, Isabella."

She did not answer him. She pulled up the corner of his bedding and wiggled quickly under and flattened herself against him and held him in a strong warmth.

"You should not do this." It was difficult to talk clearly, he was so cold.

"Agh! I did it before, many times, when we thought in the night the life would go out of your body. I felt that I held it there, and it could not go out of your cold body if I held it very tightly. And you see, it did not."

"This is a different kind of sickness. You will get it from me."

"No. I am never sick."

Still he shivered. She made a small sound of exasperation and held him the tighter, entwining his legs, rubbing his back with her hand, pulling his head down into the warm place between her throat and shoulder. Yet still he was cold. She released him, fumbled with the front of his shirt and opened it to the waist. She did something to her own night garment. Then she held him as before, and their bodies, bare from throat to waist, were pressed tightly and warmly together, and he could feel the round firm breasts against him.

"Now," she said. "Now be warm, pobrecito, pobrecito, muñeco mio."

Slowly then, the cold began to leave his body. The continual shivering turned to spasms that came less frequently, and were less severe. His teeth no longer chattered. And he feared that when at last he was warm, she would leave him. He wanted her to be with him in this way, to feel the lift and touch of her unbraided hair on his forehead as she breathed, to feel the pressing firmness of the warm body. His hand was on her waist. He wanted to caress her, but did not dare for fear she would leave. Moment by moment he became more conscious of her as a woman in his arms. He had not held a woman in a long time. In a previous existence he had held a woman, but never in this one.

Slowly he began to sense that she was as aware as he was, that there was a controlled tension about her. He dared then, to make the hand that rested on her waist tighten slightly. Her breathing changed, seeming to become slightly deeper as it quickened. He could not tell if it was something he imagined. And then there was an odd sensation against his chest, a curious sort of movement that at first he could not identify. Then suddenly, with joy and knowledge and certainty of what would come, he realized that her breasts were swelling and tightening against him. He kissed her throat and she uttered a long whispering sigh with a catch in her breath at the end of it.

The children slept. The moon came down through the hole in the thatch. The straw of the shared pallet shifted, rustled. There came from her lips a quick thin sound of shock and pain, a sharp intake of breath. There was a long silence in the night. Then, slowly, there began a pattern in the barely audible rustle of the pallet, a rhythm as old as the earth and as old as the sea, the rhythm of fruitfulness and the deep promise of life.

In the remote glow of the false dawn he heard the flap of the hanging goat skin, and he opened his eyes. Armando stood three feet inside the door and looked toward him. It seemed to Lloyd that Armando was looking directly into his eyes, though the light was so vague he knew that could not be possible. He was painfully aware of the sleeping dark head so close to his own, her breath in his ear, a shock of the black hair across his throat. And there was enough light to see the emptiness of her pallet.

Armando then walked, without sound, into the next room.

When Lloyd awakened again the sun was well up, the hut empty. He got up. He felt slightly weak, but recovered. The episode with Isabella did not seem entirely real. But there was blood on the coarse cotton pallet cover that testified to its reality. He was shocked at himself, deeply ashamed at this terribly trite and time-honored method of rewarding hospitality.

When Isabella and Concha came back to the hut to give him his noon meal, it was evident there was strain in the air. Neither of them would look directly at him. There was a small amount of stilted conversation and small rigid smilings. He ate without appetite. He could not get Isabella alone. Finally he went off to his private place in the rocks. He could feel the mountain sun baking the illness out of him. Afterward he risked the icy torrent of the waterfall, scrubbed himself half raw on the harshness of the serape.

As he walked toward the hut, he saw Armando coming

from the far fields much earlier than usual, and alone. He waited for him and said, "I would like to talk to you about a certain thing."

"Yes. We must talk. It is necessary."

"I must say that—"

Armando stopped him with a wave of his hand. "First I will talk to Isabella and to Concha, Señor Lloyd. If you would await me at the private place where you take the bath of the sun?"

"Of course."

He waited for an hour. Armando appeared and sat beside him on a flat rock where they both looked out over the valley.

"Señor, I have done a bad thing."

"Por favor, I will talk. I will speak of what is a bad thing and what is a good thing and what is a thing of no importance. Here." He took out a pint bottle of muddy mescal, pulled the cork with his teeth, handed it to Lloyd. Lloyd drank and passed it back. Armando drank, offered it again, and when Lloyd refused, recorked it and put it on the rock between them with care.

"You have no wife."

"No."

"Here we cannot give Isabella the life a woman should have. In Pinal Blanco she would be a wife of two years, perhaps heavy with a second child."

"Perhaps."

"She cared for you the most of anyone. I am a selfish man. I did not want this problem in my house. But to her it was necessary. The love came from the caring, I think."

"The love?"

"She has loved you deeply. Only a fool would not see that. You have become strong. This thing has been expected."

"It would not have happened if—"

"Then of course it would have happened in some other way for some other reason. I must act as a father in this, you understand."

"I understand."

"But I am not a fool. I know a little of the world. Often I marveled at the norteamericanos, those of the pale faces and the great gleaming automobiles and the millions of pesos and the boxes for the taking of pictures. They have stopped in the village. I am a peasant from a tiny village, Señor Lloyd. I am a man of truly great ignorance. I thought they could not be of the race of man, those pale ones. Not a man as I am a man. That discloses my ignorance. You are the first I have known and have spoken to. You live in my house. You are sympatico. You have the courtesy. You do not fear work. You do not weep when in pain. You are a man as I am a man."

"Thank you."

"Why is there thanks for telling a true thing? I have learned you are a man. I am ignorant, but there are certain practical things I can find in my head. This is not your world. You fell into this world. You will return to your place, in time. So I would be more than ignorant to say to you that it is necessary for you to marry Isabella and live here with us all your life, no? What type of marriage is that? An important norteamericano, tall as a tree, and of many years of education to marry a little peasant girl from a tiny and unimportant village! No. It is unthinkable. But there is this problem. She is the girl who loves you. To be with you, as in the night, is a good thing for her. A child would be a good thing. She knows you must go, and we all know of the thing you must do. It makes a problem. I could say to you and to Isabella, live with each other until he must go. Then what? We are cut off from the church it is true. But we are a good people. Such a thing is only right if, as in the village, marriage must be delayed. Now I do not beg. I only ask. I have spoken of this to Roberto, Rosario, Concha and Isabella. There could be here this thing we call a marriage. A place could be built for you. Then when you leave and go back to your own place, it can be in your mind that it never happened. It is not a thing of law. The reading of the words by Roberto does not make something to hold you here, or keep you from making a marriage in your own country. Do you understand. It will be easier for everyone. She is a good strong girl. It will give her a part of life perhaps she could not have in any other way. And, after you have left, if it is done this way, then the other women cannot make her feel shame. Her or the child. Before you speak, there is one more thing, Señor Lloyd. It will make cause for a fiesta. Do not answer. Drink from the bottle. Then think. And then answer."

It was a curious and eminently fair proposition. Armando had thought it out well. It could not be more fair to all concerned.

"Yes," Lloyd said.

Armando beamed at him. "I will tell her," he said.

"No, Tio. No es correcto. I will *ask* her. And first we shall drink this small amount remaining. There is not enough to save, do you think?"

"Not enough."

It was the wrong time of year for the building of huts. Yet, after Lloyd and Isabella selected the spot, everyone stopped all other tasks and worked together, and it was finished in a week. They had the wedding the day after the completion of the hut. Isabella was in white, her braids gleaming, her eyes downcast, her hand locked in Lloyd's. Roberto read the words in impressive and sonorous fashion. Concha wept. After the pronouncement, they got up from their knees and he kissed her. Before the kiss was finished, they heard the first tentative strum of the guitar. Roberto had made a special trip and brought in pulque, mescal and tequila. Lloyd got extremely drunk. He remembered reciting to all of them, in English, and with gestures never used before, the only two poems he knew by heart, 'The Lady of Shalott' and 'The Wasteland'. He remembered deciding that the Eliot line about the thousand lost golf balls had probably never been recited under more incongruous circumstances. Both contributions were enthusiastically applauded. Later, when he demonstrated the American custom of carrying the bride across the threshold, he lurched and thumped her head solidly against the edge of the door. She said, rubbing her head, that under those circumstances she could not understand how American women could endure to be married so many times.

In the next two months he told himself that this was just a peasant girl, a village girl. But there was no peasant dullness to her mind or her wit. When angered or hurt—and that was seldom—she changed utterly. Her face lost all expression. It became a round Indio mask, implacable as though carved in stone, with only the glint of obsidian eyes to show the quick life behind the mask. She could be monstrously stubborn. She had a great loyalty to him. It was clear she would die for him if it should become necessary, yet this devotion in no way turned her into a serf. She had both dignity and a sense of honor. She was not a paragon. She was a most human person, an individual, with depths that defied complete knowing. She moved quickly, and with such a deftness that he could not tire of watching her.

By the standards of his prior life, her body was not attractive. She was perhaps five foot three inches tall and weighed one hundred and twenty five. In no place was she fragile or delicate. Yet there was no part of her where she was too heavy or thickened. There was a rubbery suppleness about her—a texture of work muscles knit tightly over bone and overlayed with an even distribution of fat to give her a woman's softness. She could be as playful as a brown bear cub, and at those times she was like a child. Her body was the shade of strong coffee with cream, and downy as any peach. He would think of her as a squat and chunky little woman, and then, in the wavery yellow light of the precious kerosene flame he would see the bold and thrusting roundness of a breast, or the modeling of a haunch, or the smooth rounded flow of belly into loins and know this figure was classic in the heroic and historical sense. This was the very essence of woman, more enduring than the bloodlessness of *Vogue,* more vital and meaningful than the self-induced anemia of *Harper's Bazaar.*

After an initial shyness, physical love was, to her, as natural and as necessary as the clean mountain air she breathed, the food she fixed for them. She made her need known to him with a frankness that was neither boldness nor impudence. He would walk out and watch her in the last light of day, washing clothing in the cold brook, braids swinging, face closed in her Indian mask of determination, and he would think her a stranger, someone he could not possibly understand. Then later in darkness she would be in his arms, and her body would be a complete miracle, and he would think that never had he been closer to another human being.

With the change of the season and the coming of the first warmth, the tempo of work increased as they began the planting. He had become as tireless as the others, muscles tough as braided leather, brown of hide. He had never been more fit. With his bigger frame, he was stronger than the others. And took a curious primitive pride in his strength. He wondered if he was turning into a vegetable, willing to forego the lack of any mental stimulation. He had no idea of what was happening in the world, and no special desire to know. Sometimes in the evening he would sit with the men and they would look out over the valley and talk of the great and simple mysteries.

One night Isabella took his hand and placed it on the round warmth of her belly and said, "We have created a small creature."

"After great labors," he said, smiling into the dark of the room.

"Which, of course, were not enjoyed. I am wondering about him. He is maybe the size of a beetle, or perhaps even as huge as a mouse."

"Does he have a name?"

"Not yet. He is too small for a name. But he has a great ugly beard and a taste for mescal."

After a long silence she said, "How soon will you leave?"

"Soon."

"But when?"

"When the planting is finished."

A day or so later, as she was cooking, he said, after much thought, "I could stay here until he is born, Isabella."

She whirled and stared at him. He expected gladness. She spoke in a voice of shrillness and tension. "Ah, yes! And then wait for the next one also. And perhaps their children too. And that beard will be white and you will say to the other men, 'One day I will leave to do this thing I must do.' Then they will grin behind your back and they will say to their women that Isabella prevented Lloyd from living as a man. Go! Go soon, and do not come back to this place. It is *my* child. One day when he can understand, I can tell him a true thing about his father and make him proud."

He left three days later, dressed in the suit Isabella had saved, hair carefully cut, beard trimmed, feet uncomfortable in shoes, and carrying a suitcase, the one that had survived with least damage. He felt ridiculous straddling the small burro which followed Roberto's burro. He looked back at them standing there and lifted an arm in salute. Isabella stood with closed face, with the Indian look. Their stormy farewell had been said in private. A moment later they were around a corner of rock.

They reached Talascatan just before dusk. Lloyd said, "I never asked you, Roberto. How is it you are able to come here without trouble from the people of Pinal Blanco?"

"I was not involved in the trouble. I am never involved in any trouble. This is for you. It is from the people of the valley. It is a very old thing."

It was a dagger with ornate handle, dull silver sheath, slim and deadly blade. There was an inscription on the blade, difficult to read. Roberto said, "It says there, 'I tickle the heart of wickedness.' "

"Thank you. And thank all the others."

"We will remember you."

"There are some small things I would send them. How can that be arranged?"

"Send them to a man with the name Osvaldo Morella of Talascatan. That is his store over there. He is honest. I shall tell him something will be sent."

"I was not blindfolded, Roberto."

He grinned. "It was not considered necessary."

"On that highest part where it is narrow, I would have preferred a blindfold."

"One merely closes the eyes. The burro has no fear. Go with God, my friend."

He spent two nights at Zimapan. On the second night he was able to move into the room where he had hidden the money. He recovered it without incident. He moved into a small cheap hotel in Mexico City. He could not become entirely accustomed to the way people looked at him on the street, the men with curiosity, with slight shock, the women with revulsion. He learned finally the name and address of the man he should see, and made an appointment.

Dr. Eric Hausmann was an old man. He was heavy, slow and asthmatic. There were brownish blotches on his naked head, and his face fell into mournful folds. But small grey eyes were keen behind the polished lenses, and the thick white hands were steady. He studied Lloyd with professional interest, sat him under strong light, fingered the bones under the broken face. He snapped the light out and they went back to his desk. Lloyd's Spanish was far better than the doctor's English.

"You speak well," the doctor said.

"Thank you."

"You speak in the idiom of the mountain villages. It is not a cultured tongue."

"I have lived with the villagers."

"These injuries are old. Perhaps a year."

"Six days less than a year."

"No doctor attended you."

"No."

"You have remarkable recuperative powers, Mr. Smith."

"Thank you."

"No one can make of you a handsome man."

"I accept that. I want to become less conspicuous."

"There are three major things to be done. The left cheek bone is badly crushed. After X-ray I can tell if the bone can be cut free and pinned in place. The nose is simpler. I can take a flap of flesh from your shoulder. Then it would be best if another man can work on the teeth while you are under anaesthetic. What more will you require?"

"What more can you do?"

"The jaw has healed crookedly in two places. But not much would be gained. It has knitted well. The beard disguises the crookedness. There is minor surgery that could be performed on the lips. I can make the forehead scar less apparent."

"Perhaps just the scar on the forehead, and this one place on the upper lip."

"That can be done. It will be expensive. And you must expect pain."

"I have become accustomed to pain."

"That is understandable, Mr. Smith. Do you have a picture of yourself, taken before your . . . accident?"

"I would prefer not to be recognized as myself."

Hausmann nodded as though he had expected that answer. He wrote figures on a piece of paper. He added the figures. "Depending on how quickly you heal, Mr. Smith, you will be in the hospital—a small private institution where I do most of my work—from six to eight weeks. This figure I will give you includes that time, and my fee, and the estimated fee of the dental surgeon, including the dentures you will need. Thirty-five thousand pesos will cover everything."

Below the edge of the desk, Lloyd counted out a thousand dollars. He put it on the desk. "May I give you this now?"

"Thank you. When will you be prepared to enter the hospital? The X-rays will be taken there."

"Will Monday be convenient?"

Hausmann wrote the name and address of the hospital.

"Be at this place at nine o'clock on Monday morning. I will make all of the arrangements."

During the three days he had allowed himself, Lloyd made extensive arrangements to provide essentials for the settlement in the valley. It would have been impossible for him to manage without his fluency in the language. He knew what was needed. All of his purchases were packed into twenty-two wooden crates, of a size Roberto could transport by burro over the mountain trails. He found a man of honesty who owned a truck and he paid him well to take the crates to the store of Osvaldo Morella in Talascatan to be held there for Roberto to pick up. And, through the truck driver, he sent a gift of money to Morella. He could imagine the excitement that would accompany the opening of each crate as Roberto brought them, one or two at a time, from Talascatan. Two of the crates were for Isabella and the unborn child, and were so marked. At the very last, he added a twenty-third crate containing tequila, mescal and fireworks, the raw materials for fiesta.

He put the balance of his money in a lock box in a Mexico City bank. Then he was ready for the hospital.

Six weeks later when the last bandages were removed, he was allowed to sit up and look at himself in strong light, in the mirror held by a pretty smiling nurse. Hausmann stood by the foot of the bed.

Lloyd saw a face he had never seen before. The vivid patch of white hair was still there, but it was muted now by a greyness that had spread over his entire head. The reddish beard, just beginning to grow back, was touched with grey. Under the thin beard he could see the two kinds of scars, the ugly ones made by rock, and the thin neat pink lines drawn by Hausmann's scalpel. The left cheek was somewhat distorted, but the sick hollow was gone. The jaw was irregular. The great scar on the forehead was miraculously muted. Only the eyes and the shape of the brow were reminiscent of a man he had once known, yet in this stranger's face, that look of familiarity was slight.

"You were correct," he said. "I shall never be handsome."

"When the beard is heavier it will be better," Hausmann said.

"Then you will look interesting," the nurse said, smiling.

"You have done a good job, Dr. Hausmann," Lloyd said.

"How do the teeth feel?"

"Uncomfortable."

"You will become accustomed to them. Mine were removed in Hamburg in 1934, with a rifle butt, the few I had left at that time."

On the fifth day of August a very tall and very drunken American walked across the bridge from Matamoros into Brownsville, Texas. He wore a white suit and the right hand pocket sagged with the weight of the half empty bottle of rum. He had a ragged straw hat, of the sort that tourists buy, shoved well back on his head. He had a heavy reddish brown beard, and a look of awkward, uncoordinated strength. The petty officials on the Mexican side watched his wavering progress with bored, cynical amusement.

He argued loudly and profanely with the officials on the American side, complaining how they misused tourists in the dives of Matamoros, and mispronouncing Mexican words. He said that the others, his friends who had driven him over to the town, could damn well stay over there. He was going back to the hotel, by God. They told him he better take one of the cabs parked near the bridge. He had the driver let him out in the center of the city. The driver marveled to himself at how a man so drunk could pull himself together so quickly. Later the driver found the half bottle of rum in the back of the cab. The American must have been very drunk after all to have forgotten his rum.

The tall American checked into a hotel and, having no luggage, paid in advance. When the room door was locked, he sat in a chair by the windows and looked out at what he could see of the city by night. He had the clothes he wore. He had a little over two hundred Mexican pesos. And, in two money belts, and distributed in various pockets, he had almost exactly thirty thousand dollars.

7

Lloyd knew that any successful execution was a complicated thing to arrange. He had long since ceased calling it murder. In this case it was particularly complicated. The entire problem would be simplified if he were willing to sacrifice himself along with his elected victims. Yet, in spite of his hate, in spite of the necessity of this thing, he wished to continue to live, wished to be quite safe after it was over. In that way the details of the execution could be savored again and again.

Before specific plans could be drawn up, certain major problems required consideration. He would have to acquire a reasonably fool-proof identity. And, in that new identity, he would have to acquire a new set of habits and mannerisms. He had never been fingerprinted, so that was one problem he did not have to consider. With his tallness, and the beard, the visible scars and the patch of dead white hair, he would be easily remembered. That was another factor in the equation.

In order to get close to Tulsa, Benny and Harry Danton he would have to be at the Hotel Green Oasis. There was enough money so he could go there as a guest. Yet, as a guest, he did not feel he would have as many opportunities as he would as an employee. Obviously, many of the people he had hired, and had worked closely with, would still be there. A new face and new mannerisms might not be enough. He remembered the other hotels under construction at the time he left. There were certain possibilities in that direction.

He wrote the biography of a man named Robert Rose. He made a chronological account of his life, using his own date of birth. He worked on it a long time, trying to account in logical ways for the failure of Robert Rose to have a social security number, any bonding company record, any union affiliation, and still have hotel experience. For a long time he could not solve this problem. The final solution pleased him. He had been born and educated in the states. His father owned and operated a hotel in Mexico. His father had become a Mexican citizen, but Robert Rose had retained his American citizenship. Robert had worked in the hotel. Recently his father had died and the hotel had been sold. That would account for the money in his possession, and the lack of records. His damaged face could be blamed on Korea. No. That would mean a cross-checking of records by the bonding company. It had been a highway accident in Mexico. And he could use his fluent Mexican Spanish to prove his background.

He went to Houston. He acquired a used car, a driver's license, a hunting license, and all other manner of identification he could acquire. He destroyed the last bits of paper that proved he was Lloyd Wescott. He practiced pitching his voice lower, and speaking more slowly. He moved more slowly. He rented a furnished room. He practiced his story until he could tell it calmly and naturally, with just enough detail to make it sound true. By the time he acquired a job in an almost firstrate hotel, as a desk man on the night shift, his money was down to less than twenty-seven thousand. He was taken on trial. He got his social security card. He filled out the blank for the bonding company. He was approved. He did his work well. The manager was pleased with him. In late January, when there was a vacancy, he was given a raise and put on the noon to eight shift. He made no friends. He was competent, uncommunicative. He tried at all times to make his new identity real to himself. His success was only partial. It seemed to him that he had lost any real identity. Lloyd

Wescott was dead. The husband of Isabella no longer existed. Sometimes he wondered if he was close to madness, if in the fall he had taken, there had been some traumatic disarrangement.

He resigned in March.

On the fifth day of April, Robert Rose opened a large checking account in the Bank of Oasis Springs, and dealt with the same official who had opened an account back in another lifetime for a man named Lloyd Wescott. He opened the account with a check drawn on a Houston bank.

"Are you a new resident, Mr. Rose?"

"I'm going to look for work here. Hotel work."

"I'm sure you'll find it without any trouble. Oasis Springs is the new Las Vegas, you know."

"I've heard that."

"The Safari opened last month. It's an enormous place. Sign again here, please. In three days you can draw checks on the account, Mr. Rose. We appreciate your business."

He walked out to the car. There had been no flicker of interest, beyond what one would normally expect. He drove through the town. The twenty-two months had brought many changes. He drove slowly out to the Hotel Green Oasis. The sign had been changed. It was huge, garish and vulgar. The plantings were scraggly and areas of the lawns were parched. He noted that new banks of floodlights had been installed on the grounds. At night the hotel must blaze like a beacon. He drove by it three times before he found the necessary courage.

The manager was not in. He waited for over an hour in the lobby. The clientele had changed. These people were flashier, and they walked and talked with all the arrogance of the insecure. The house had a shabby look. The lobby carpeting needed replacement. Maintenance seemed practically non-existent. There were few familiar faces among the help. The bell captain was the same, as were two of the cashiers, one of the desk men, one of the elevator operators. He could sense that the house wasn't full. And there was a listlessness about the help.

It was a slack house and would require months of concentrated work if it were to recover. The salvaging of the reputation would take much longer. Perhaps that could never be redeemed.

Finally he was told the manager would see him. As he went through he was glad to see that neither Mrs. Boyer nor Betty Larkin, his secretary, were there. It was unlikely they would still be with the hotel. The manager was named Tremaine, and his secretary was a big sultry brunette in too tight a dress. Tremaine was a small man with a continental accent, a small shiny mustache, a slightly wilted flower in his buttonhole, and a manner of great self-importance. Lloyd had seen the type before. They bustled through the third- and fourth-class hotels of Europe and the second-class hotels of America. They were seedy, multi-lingual, arrogant, and as dishonest as their uncertain nerve would permit them to be. They made a servile fuss over nobility of equal seediness, and cockroaches flourished in all of their kitchens.

Tremaine looked over the credentials of Robert Rose. He asked questions in a cold and haughty manner. "I can't possibly use you in front, Rose. I'm completely staffed." He scribbled on a piece of paper. "Take this to a Mr. Haglund. At this time of day you may find him in the kitchens. Tell him to speak to me if he thinks he can use you."

Once he was back out in the lobby, he nearly left. This was going to be very risky. He had worked closely with Jack Haglund. Together they had made the food served anywhere in the Hotel Green Oasis exceptional. Haglund had been one of his right hand men. This could be extraordinarily dangerous.

He found Jack standing at a steam table drinking coffee. The change in the man was shocking. He had put on at least twenty-five pounds, and it was puffy, unhealthy weight. Jack's fingers were yellowed, and his hand shook as he read the note from Tremaine, crumpled it in his hand. Lloyd suddenly realized Haglund was slightly drunk. His shirt and his nails were not completely clean.

"Do you know a damn thing about this business?"

"Yes, sir."

"You know what I've got to have? I've got to have a coordinator. That's the word for it. Somebody to keep things straightened away. The damn chefs and the waiters and the buying and the billing." He thumped his chest. "A personal assistant to me. Man can't handle everything himself forever. Gets tired. Think you can do it?"

"Yes, sir."

Haglund peered at him. "We ever work anywhere together, Rose?"

"I don't believe so."

"If you're no damn good, I'll soon find out."

Lloyd worked hard for a week. He knew he was being watched. He knew the food staff was suspicious of him. He learned the routine, avoiding the traps. Haglund did practically nothing. The kitchens were dirty, the food indifferently prepared. Dining room service was insolent. Inventory control was sloppy. Many of the good systems he and Haglund had worked out long ago had been altered or dropped. The thieving was highly organized. It was impossible not to learn of it. Every crooked device was being employed. Headwaiters soothed the customers who spotted the errors on their checks. The dining room cashiers split with the waiters. Kitchen staffs had almost unlimited opportunity for pilferage. And Jack Haglund took a percentage of every theft in addition to the kickbacks on his purchasing. Lloyd did not think of improvements. He tried only to make it run smoothly within the framework of theft and indifference.

At the end of ten days Haglund had him come to his small littered office. He put a bottle of the best bonded bourbon, two glasses and a silver ice bucket on his desk top.

"Fix yourself one, Robert."

"Thank you, sir."

"The name is Jack."

"Then thank you, Jack."

Haglund made a drink. "What do you think of the operation?"

Lloyd shrugged.

"You know this business. You know the score. What do you think of the operation?"

"It stinks."

"The whole house stinks. It loses money. And nobody gives a damn because the Casino makes enough to take care of the owners. Over here in the house we take care of ourselves. The customers are too tight to give a damn if we poison them or charge them double. There's no repeat business anyway. What I want to know is this. Will you ride with it?"

"For how much?"

"Good question. You're smart, Robert Rose. And I've seen you someplace before, damn it."

"I don't think so."

"Skip that. You got any ideas?"

Lloyd knew what he meant. Ideas that would improve Haglund's particular operation. "The bar control is still good, and the check totals on drinks are accurate. You've got space out back to set up a service bar for the dining room. Then your waiters would know which tables they could pad for an extra round. And you could go short on the drinks."

"We don't get too much drink trade in the dining room."

"It'll add up to more than you think, Jack."

"Maybe I'll give it a try. What do you want?"

"Something on the side. Whatever you want to make it. And I want to live in."

Jack gave him fifty dollars, five tens. "You're working out fine, Robert. You're using your head."

"Thank you."

"I'll get you fixed up with a room over in the wing. You can live a little better on the inside."

"I know."

"It's easier to line up something."

As Lloyd got up to leave, Haglund said foggily, "Just don't think it was always this way or I was always this way. We had a good house here in the beginning. We had a hell of a good manager. Wescott. You maybe heard of him."

"Yes, I have."

"I ought to get out of here, I guess. Most of the others left. The good ones. This operation is falling apart." He looked up, frowning. "But there's no harm getting it while you can, is there?"

"No."

"So I'm living good. That's the angle. Live good. Wescott was almost as tall as you are."

"I've got to get back."

"You're doing a good job."

The next day he was given a room with private bath in the wing where staff members lived. He moved his gear in. Haglund made an adjustment in his working hours. From his windows he could see the heavy screen of plantings in front of Harry's cottage and office. It was on the third day he was in his room, at four in the afternoon, just before he had to go back on duty, that he saw Harry Danton. Two years had made no change in him. He came walking from the cottage with a tall blonde girl. They were obviously arguing. The girl was making angry gestures. She wore a dark red sheath bikini of some shiny material that looked metallic. He saw her wince when Harry took her arm, and saw the anger go out of her. She turned and went back toward the cottage. Harry watched her go, and then walked slowly toward the hotel and was soon out of sight of the window. Lloyd realized his hands had become fists. His nails had made dents in the palms of his hands. His fingers were cramped. He rubbed the tension out of them.

Two days later Benny and Tulsa came into the kitchens a little after ten at night. Lloyd was sitting at a table checking master copies of menus. They sat fifteen feet away and began talking to one of the chefs. Lloyd gathered from the conversation they had just come back from a trip to New York. Tulsa was as big and powerful as before. He looked slightly heavier, and his hair had receded further. Benny had gained more weight around the middle.

He heard Tulsa say, "Who's the beard over there?"

"New assistant to Haglund."

"Has he got a name?"

"Robert Rose."

It seemed normal to look over when he heard his name. "You, with the beard," Tulsa said. "You ever work in Detroit?"

"No. Why?"

"I thought maybe you just worked in Detroit once. How come the spinach?"

"My beard? I'm scarred up."

Tulsa got up and came over and stood looking down at him.

"You always had the beard?"

"Since I was twenty-two. Who are you?"

"I'm Tulsa. I work for Harry. So does Benny over there. Benny, you ever see this joker before?"

Benny studied him. "Never did."

"And who is Harry?" Lloyd asked.

"Hey, Benny! He wants to know who Harry is."

"Harry is Harry Danton who owns the joint," Benny said.

Lloyd shrugged and went back to work. Tulsa went back to the table. They talked in a low tone. Lloyd could not hear them. That night, back in his room, he sat in his underwear shorts on the side of the bed. He took the knife Roberto had given him, the knife he had carried out of Mexico strapped to his body. He tested its sharpness again by shaving a small place on the outside of his thigh. He thought of the motel room in Talascatan, of the sounds that had come through the closed door. He remembered the zopilotes and the cairn of stones. He recalled vividly the white smashing explosions of pain and the stink of his own chest.

He could not sleep that night. The time had come for the specific plans. He made his selection. The first one would be Benny. And Benny Bernholz had a fear of heights. He had wanted Valerez to be first, but he had not seen Valerez and could not ask about him. It was probable that Valerez was still in Mexico. The first step would be to acquire Benny's confidence and trust. That would not be easy. It would never be given to anyone in full measure. He needed to win that confidence, because death was not enough. There had to be the awareness, the comprehension of the identity of the executioner, and there was a breaking point that had to come before death.

Now that Benny and Tulsa were back, Benny was often in the kitchens, getting in the way, demanding special service. The original prop was very simple. Lloyd searched the news stands of Oasis Springs and acquired a thick stack of fantasy and science fiction comic books. He read them. He left them in his room, in plain sight. The next time he saw Benny reading one of his comic books, he moved to where he could look over Benny's shoulder. He stood there until Benny turned and glared up in annoyance. "What the hell you doing?"

"Let me see it a minute," Lloyd said calmly and picked it up, looked at the cover. "This is a pretty good one."

Benny's annoyance disappeared. "Hey! You go for this stuff too? How about in here where they get this injection that turns you into a plant like?"

"That's pretty good. I've got a bunch of them in my room."

"You have? How about the lend of them, Rosie?"

"Go on up and read them any time. I don't like to loan them out. Go on up now if you want. Here's the key."

He knew that would be disarming. Benny could find nothing in the room out of character. The knife was safely hidden. And there was a chance Benny would look at the balance in his checking account. The check book was in the top drawer of the bureau.

"Bring me back the key when you're through. I get off in about an hour and a half."

When he went up to the room Benny was sprawled on his bed, reading. He grinned at Lloyd when he came in and closed the door. "You got some good stuff here. You want to sleep or something, I'll clear out."

"Stick around."

Benny read, and then he wanted to talk. He wanted to tell the best plots he could remember. He wanted to tell them in considerable detail. Then they played some gin. Lloyd played as poorly as he could. Benny won readily. When Lloyd said he was ready to quit, Benny was disappointed.

"You seem to be a quiet type guy, Rosie."

"That's the best way."

"I like to live it up some."

"I used to."

"So what happened?"

"You ask a hell of a lot of questions."

"Don't get sore. Me and Tulsa were talking about you."

"So?"

"He says you act like you're carrying a little heat."

"Could be."

"So you're keeping your head down. Is that it?"

"Could be."

"This your regular kind of work?"

"It used to be."

"It's a handy thing to have a trade. A job is a good place to go cool off, like. You're among friends, Rosie. What kind of a deal was it?"

"You still ask too many questions."

"So you don't answer them, I go tell Harry you're hot. It makes him nervous."

"I'd tell you to go to hell, Benny. But I've got a problem."

"So?"

"I don't want everybody and his brother in on it. I don't want Tulsa and Harry in on it. I've got to have one contact. That's all I need. I was working a deal in Miami. A hotel deal. I was on the desk. So I case the guests. When they're loaded, I get the name and home town. I was working with two friends. They would call the guests and say that so and so in the home town had asked them to have the guests out to a dinner party while they were in Miami. You can take the front name right out of Dun and Bradstreet. If the guests won't play, then my friend would say it was probably the wrong Joneses or Andersons or whatever. But if they fall for it—and you only use people with their own car—they get directions that take them about fifteen miles out of Miami. To a dark place. There they get jumped and stripped of everything. The car is disabled. My friends come back fast and I give them a room key and they work the room over."

Benny had been listening eagerly. "Nice!" he said.

"We worked it a dozen times and then the cops got too close and grabbed my friends. I picked up the stuff and left."

"You fenced it?" Lloyd knew from that question that Benny had seen the bank balance.

"No."

"What have you got? Furs? Ice? Stuff like that?"

"That's right."

"Not here, for God's sake?"

"I'm not that stupid."

"Harry wouldn't want stuff like that around. We keep this place clean. Give them half a chance and they lift your licenses and then you're dead. Where is it?"

"In a safe place. I want to unload it."

"Do you have any idea how much it's worth, say at retail?"

"Maybe a hundred and fifty thousand. There's five mink coats, and a couple of sable wraps. Diamond clips. One small string of matched pearls. One emerald ring that looks good. And a lot of junk. Watches, things like that."

"What do you want out of it, Rosie?"

"What kind of a deal can you make?"

"I got a couple of contacts. But if they come this far and it's no sale, then they get sore at me, see? I'd want to see the stuff first. What kind of an end do I get?"

"If you make all the arrangements and get me the money in nothing over a fifty, you can have twenty-five percent."

He saw the flush of greed on Benny's face, the new brightness of his eyes. "What if the offer my friend makes is low?"

"I'm tired of sitting on the stuff. Make this just you and me, though. Don't bring anybody else in."

"Harry don't like for us to have anything working on the side."

"This is different. This is just a business arrangement. I'd be paying you for a service."

"That's right. But Harry would be sore anyway."

"He doesn't find out from me. Unless you try to cross me. Then he finds out."

Benny thought it over. "My friend will take his expenses off."

"That's all right. How do you get hold of him?"

"I can make a call from down in town. First I got to see the stuff, Rosie. Where is it?"

"I can take you to it."

"Where is it? In storage?"

"I'll take you to it. We can drive to where it is. It will take an hour and a half to get there and back. We shouldn't be seen taking off together. How about five o'clock tomorrow morning? All right with you?"

"Okay."

"See you in the parking lot."

Lloyd had located the place a week previously, had purchased what he needed and had left it there, well hidden. It was not in an area of big mountains. The road that led to the spot was a mere trace, winding between rocks. The actual drop was steep, one hundred feet he estimated, to the bed of the dry arroyo. It was an area of baked rock, the shimmer of mirage and the quickness of lizards. The featurelessness of the land dwarfed the drop. A single tough and stunted tree, close to death, grew at the brink of the drop, roots reaching down into the cracks in the rock for traces of moisture that had sustained it.

They had driven toward the sunrise, and no car was in sight when Lloyd turned off the highway. The car jounced and rocked as he followed the trace, and Benny said, "What the hell, Rosie?"

"The stuff is in a good safe place. I'll show you. It's not far from here."

He came to a relatively smooth place where he could go a bit faster. Out of the corner of his eye he saw Benny leaning forward, looking ahead. He stamped the brake pedal hard. Benny's head thudded the windshield so hard it made radial cracks. He sagged back, not quite unconscious, making slow movements like a man under water. An automatic appeared in his hand, flat and blue. Lloyd drove his right fist against the corner of the jaw twice, and twisted the gun out of Benny's hand. Benny still stirred weakly and subsided when Lloyd hit him across the side of the head with the barrel of the weapon. He drove another two hundred feet, parked and pulled Benny out of the car. He carried him to the edge of the drop, then went and got the heavy length of rope from the place where he had hidden it. He tied it firmly around Benny's chest, under the armpits, and ran a single loop under the crotch and fastened it in back. He tossed the free end of the line over a thick limb that stuck out over the dropoff at about a forty-five degree angle. He retrieved the dangling end with a long stick. A secondary limb kept the rope from sliding back to the trunk. He walked the rope back and made it fast to a stout outcropping of rock that slanted away from the brink. He pushed Benny over the edge. Benny jolted hard at the end of the rope, swung out, swung back and hit the face of the drop-off lightly and then continued to swing, face down, arms and legs dangling. He hung too low. Lloyd braced himself and pulled him higher, looping the line around the outcropping each time he had enough slack. When Benny hung four feet below the limb, he stopped. He was breathing hard with the exertion. He sat and leaned his back against the tree. Benny swung gently back and forth and finally came to rest.

He was a grotesque sight, a small stocky man with bald spot and clown face, with dark green slacks and yellow sports shirt, with brown and white shoes. He belonged at the corner of Broadway and Forty-fifth, nursing a cigar, watching the women, digesting strawberry cheesecake. He did not belong in a barren land, strung up in the hot slant of morning sunlight, looking curiously like bait set out to tempt some unimaginable creature.

Lloyd tried to feel satisfaction, to feel the hot delight of the avenger. But all he could feel was a tiredness, and a rather plaintive sympathy for the little man with his pointed and perforated shoes.

The right hand moved first. It lifted tentatively toward the face and dropped again. He saw the eyes open slowly and close, open slowly and close again, and then spring wide open, dilating with horror. The arms and legs made curiously frantic swimming motions and the body tensed. Then the motions started him swinging and the body became rigid, the eyes clenched shut. His breathing was loud and fast.

The eyes opened again and the head turned with great caution and Benny looked into his eyes. Benny's face was a strange pasty green under the sunburn. "Christ!" he said. "Good Christ!"

"I been wondering about those comic books, Benny. Have you got your anti-grav hooked up?"

"Rosie, for Christ' sake!"

"Nearly all of those people can fly." The unsheathed dagger made a silvery flash in the sunlight. Lloyd rested the cutting edge against the taut rope. "The way to teach a kid to swim is throw him into the water, Benny. I want to teach you how to fly."

Benny screamed. He screamed with each breath he took and then hung slack, eyes closed. He turned his head slowly and Lloyd saw him swallow. "Look, Rosie," he said pleadingly. "I can't really fly. Honest. It won't work."

"How do we know unless we try?"

"Rosie, you're sick or something. Honest. Get me back. We'll go have a beer. No hard feelings."

"That wouldn't be fair. We didn't go have a beer the other time, Benny."

"What other time? *Who are you?*"

"You remember, Benny. Sure you do. You and Tulsa and Valerez. Tulsa killed Sylvia. Then you shoved us over the cliff in the car."

Benny stared unbelievingly. His mouth worked. "Wescott," he whispered. "You couldn't live through that. I . . . I saw you. That thing was a mile deep."

"Lloyd Wescott, Benny. All ready to teach you how to fly."

"Hold it! Wait. Lloyd, for Christ sake! What do you want? Look! Let me buy out. This won't do you no good. I know how you feel. You want to get Tulsa and Harry too. Let me help you with them. You got to have help. You can't do it alone. Look, I'll help you nail both of them and I'll give you twenty-five thousand bucks. I swear on my mother's grave, I won't cross you. Look, we had to do like Harry said. I always liked you. Honest, I felt bad having to do you like that. It was orders."

"You were crying while you were burning me."

"That was Tulsa. He's half nuts. He likes that stuff."

"Where can I find Valerez?"

"In hell. He got it in San Antone six months ago. It was a woman thing. Somebody put a knife in him. He lived maybe a week, but they'd cut his gut up too much. I'll help you with Tulsa, honest. And Harry too."

"Who else has Harry got hanging around, beside you and Tulsa?"

"Nobody. There's no trouble. This rope is cutting me in half, Lloyd. Wait a minute. Look. Suppose all of a sudden I disappear. Then Harry will get nervous and he'll bring some people down, just in case. Then he'll be too rough for you."

Lloyd stood up and picked up a rock as big as a basketball. He dropped it over. They watched it hit and splinter. It had seemed to fall for a long time. Benny began to scream again, eyes knotted shut, arms and legs flailing. He sagged once more, panting.

"I guess you're going to do it," he said dully. "I get all the breaks. I got all the luck."

"I'm going to do it."

"Will you do it another way?"

"What do you mean?"

"Where's my gun?"

"In the car."

"From this close you could hardly miss hitting me in the head. Then cut the damn rope."

Lloyd placed the cutting edge of the dagger against the rope. He knew he had but to make one quick hard slash. Benny would drop away. Benny watched him. Lloyd could not bring himself to slash hard. He could not make that final decisive motion. He sawed gently, tentatively. Some of the fibers parted and then one strand popped and the two ends curled back. Benny began to scream again. The sound was lost in the emptiness of the land. He screamed and his mouth frothed and his body twisted and swung and turned.

Lloyd then realized he had come a long way to learn something about himself. He had come a long way, and across more than two years to find out that he could not kill. He tried to tell himself this man was evil, that his crimes made him unfit to live. Lloyd's hatred and his anger had been the margin that sustained him, that had kept him alive. He had thought he was hardened all the way through, that he could act without mercy. But there was still a softness.

He watched Benny. The convulsions of terror went on and on. He called to him, but he could not get his attention. He realized that something inside the man had broken. He could not leave him there. He could not cut the rope. The only recourse left to him was to bring him back. He decided the simplest method was to get Benny swinging hard enough so that he could reach out and grasp a wrist or ankle. But Benny, in madness and terror, might pull him over the brink. Better, perhaps, to pull Benny up against the limb. Then he could grasp it and turn and pull himself up onto it and work his way back to the trunk.

He pulled the crazed man up. Benny caught at the limb. He half turned and hooked a leg over it. He worked his way up until he lay flat on the limb, hugging it with arms and legs, eyes shut, each breath a sob. Lloyd waited for a long time. He called to him. Benny would not respond. He was frozen there. When Lloyd tugged on the rope, Benny held the limb more tightly. It was ludicrous to have him so close to safety and have him be so unaware of it. There seemed to be only one thing to do. Benny was securely fastened to the rope. Lloyd decided to brace himself, and pull the man free of the limb, pull him back toward the trunk. If he fell he would not fall far. He would bang against the cliff face and could be pulled up from there.

He braced himself and pulled. The limb creaked. He pulled again. There was a sudden splintering crack, and both Benny and the limb fell. The sudden weight ripped the rope through his hands. Then the weight came hard against the full length of the rope. Some of the turns of rope had slipped off the outcropping, but the end was secure. The rope popped loudly and was limp in his torn hands. He heard the final sound, a fading hoarseness from a throat too punished to scream again. And a thick sound in the arroyo bed, a sound as of a ball of mud slapped against a stone wall.

He looked at the end of the rope. It had parted where he had sliced one strand with the knife. He sat for a long time. Finally he walked to where it was an easy descent to the bottom. He cut the stained rope free of the body. He walked thirty feet away and was sick. He covered the body with sand and stones. He buried the rope in another place.

At nine thirty he was at work. The kitchen sounds were loud. Waiters were laughing and talking. Over all the sounds he kept hearing that final fading shout.

8

Two full days passed before Lloyd began to come out of it. He did his work with mechanical unthinking perfection, speaking only when it was necessary to speak. During his off duty hours he went to his room and stretched out on the bed and tried to understand why this had shocked him so deeply. He had thought it would be far different. He had visualized it all so many times. But one basic thing had been left out of his calculations —the psychic aspect of killing. The bloody destruction of the human animal. The stilling of the cleverness of the brain. And he began to understand why the murderer so often gives himself away. Even if the justification seems ample, there is a dimension to murder that cannot be sensed until after the deed. He wanted to go back and look at the place where it had happened. He wanted to try to explain to someone how it had happened, and why.

He had thought himself capable of the same callousness he had experienced at their hands. He had been misled by his own hatred, and by the mores of the tough fiction he had read. The taking of a human life ran so completely counter to the concepts of morality that had been instilled in him as a child that self-revulsion was like a sickness in him. He had learned why some soldiers, in battle, cannot shoot.

The exiles from Pinal Blanco had a simpler approach. Their morality was contingent on a sense of honor and pride. Their approach to life and death was primitive. He had imagined himself capable of using their philosophy as his own. But under it he was still a boy from a small town. Death was something with a sad sick smell of flowers, and the dull gleam of bronze handles, and the solemn intonations of the minister. Death was something that happened, not something to be caused.

He did not know what he would do next. It no longer seemed necessary to him to work in this place. It no longer seemed possible to take any pride in the cleverness with which he had gotten close to the men he had wanted to kill. Even the two years of hatred seemed, in retrospect, self-conscious and shameful.

He decided that he would work here until he had found out what he should do with himself, with his life.

Ten days after the killing of Benny, he awakened and

was aware that someone was leaning over him in the darkness of his room. Before he could react, before he could feel anything except surprise, there was a great whirling flash of light inside his head.

When he awakened he was in a moving darkness. He could hear a sound of metal wheels on stone. There was softness against his face, and he smelled soiled linen. He was curled up, knees against his chest. His head throbbed. The sound of wheels stopped. He heard the sound of a heavy door shutting. Then his world tipped violently and he rolled out across a concrete floor. He sat up, surrounded by dirty sheets and towels. He saw what he had ridden in, one of the wheeled hampers used by the room maids.

Tulsa Haynes stood over him, hard fists on his hips, Indian face without expression. Harry Danton stood beside Tulsa, one step to the rear. Danton stared intently at Lloyd. He held his hand out so as to shield the bottom of Lloyd's face from his vision.

"Maybe you're right," Danton said.

"I don't see how the hell I can be. I told you just how it was. But I know I'm right."

"Get up and walk around," Harry said.

"What's this all about, Mr. Danton?"

"Get up and walk around like I told you."

"Yes, sir."

He walked around while they looked at him.

"You see it?" Tulsa asked.

"He's the same height. But he's a lot huskier. He moves slower. His voice is deeper."

"Right from the minute I saw him, I wondered about him," Tulsa said. "After Benny disappeared, I wondered some more. I didn't figure him for Wescott. I figured him as maybe somebody planted here, somebody I seen once or twice long ago. Charlie fingered him. He took a good look and said maybe Wescott. Then the more I look, the more he looks like him."

"Would Wescott be damn fool enough to come here?"

"Maybe. What happened to Benny. You want the proof?"

"Can you hammer it out of him?"

"I don't have to. Take off your socks, Wescott."

As Lloyd had only had a two hour break from duty, he had stretched out in socks, dark trousers, white shirt. He looked at Tulsa and Harry. The room had concrete walls, overhead pipes, a single heavy door. He knew it was one of the side rooms in the subbasement. He knew Tulsa would look for the burn scars on the tops of his feet and see them and know.

"Nice to see you again, Harry," he said.

Harry shook his head wonderingly. "You poor damn fool," he said. He turned sharply toward Tulsa. "You bitched it up."

"If you could have watched it, Harry, you wouldn't say so. Look at him! Look at his face. You tell me why it didn't kill him."

"You're tough to kill, kid. Thanks for coming back and giving us another chance. Did you get Benny?"

He hesitated. "Yes."

"How?" Tulsa asked.

"I dropped him off a cliff."

"Who was next?" Tulsa asked.

"You."

"And then me," Harry said. "You boys must have gotten the kid real upset. Take care of it, Tulsa."

"You want to watch?"

"I've seen it before."

Harry turned again at the door and shook his head and said, "You poor damn fool!" He left, pulling the door shut.

There were two wall lights with pull cords. Tulsa pulled the other one on. He whistled softly. He took off his khaki shirt, folded it, put it on the floor in a corner. He worked his arms and shoulders like a fighter waiting for the bell.

"Benny was a good boy," Tulsa said.

"I didn't think so."

"We been together a long time. I'm going to miss having him around. Nobody is going to miss having you around, Wescott. I'm going to make this last. I never had such a good chance to make something last. You know, we may waltz around down here for a week. Nobody's in any hurry. You in a hurry?"

Lloyd stood tensely, shifted his weight warily, turning toward Tulsa as he moved around, shadow-boxing. "Like this left jab? Lotta snap, hey? Take a good look."

The jab snapped his head back. He moved away. He wondered how much his face could stand, if the pinned bones would crush easily, if the nose would tear along the stitched line. But he knew this was a trivial consideration. Tulsa meant to kill him. Tulsa had killed Sylvia with his hands. The bare room provided no possibility of a weapon. Tulsa bounded with rubbery elasticity. He moved from side to side, feinting, clowning, grinning, and Lloyd realized he was being maneuvered into a corner.

He tried to slip away, but he could not. As Tulsa came in, he swung a right at his face as hard as he could, but it slipped over Tulsa's shoulder and again he was as helpless as he had been in the motel room at Talascatan. Tulsa wedged him into the corner, pivoting, grunting, with each blow, and it seemed that the fists were tearing holes in his body and his strength was running from those holes. As before, he sagged against the man, chin bouncing on the sweaty shoulder, teeth clacking, room dancing in his vision. He half saw the ear, a small neat folded ear, like the ear of a trim animal. He caught the rubbery texture in his teeth, ripped hard.

Tulsa leaped back with a whinnying scream, like a horse trapped in a burning barn. He clapped his hand to the torn ear. Blood ran down the side of his face. He charged, maddened with pain, throwing an overhand right which could have and should have killed Lloyd by crushing his head between fist and wall. Though sick and dazed, Lloyd managed to move his head just far enough to the right so the fist grazed his left cheek before smashing into the concrete wall with a force that burst the hard skin over the knuckles and smashed the bones of the hand.

Tulsa did not scream. He dropped to his knees. He held his right hand across his belly and folded his body over it until his face almost touched the floor. Lloyd, moving away from him, stumbled and fell. It seemed to take a long time to get up. From heart to groin he felt as though flesh had been hammered loose from bone.

He tottered over to Tulsa, raised his stockinged foot, stamped Tulsa's head against the floor. Tulsa rolled toward him, swept his feet out from underneath him, clambered onto him, found his throat with the big undamaged left hand. Lloyd had time to tense his throat muscles. Tulsa pressed his face against Lloyd's chest and the big hand tightened. Lloyd tried to get hold of one of the fingers and pry the hand open. But the fingers were strong and slippery and the tips were buried in the flesh of the side of his throat. He felt the darkness coming. He could not get a grasp on the very short dark hair in order to lift the head and reach for the eyes. The muscles of his throat were losing strength and being compressed inward. He worked his hands under the dark head, feeling for the eyes. Darkness was upon him then, but he managed to get his thumbs into the corners of the eyes. As he exerted pressure, Tulsa gasped and rolled away from him.

Lloyd was on one knee before his vision cleared enough so he could see the big shoe swinging toward his face. He grabbed the ankle and gave a twisting heave and Tulsa went down. Lloyd got up and wavered over to the wall and leaned against it, breathing hard. Tulsa turned to face him, still on his knees.

He got up very slowly. The broken hand dangled at his side. He moved toward Lloyd, left fist ready. Lloyd pushed himself away from the wall. He planted his feet. He swung at the man's face, swung leaden arms as hard as he could. He knew the blows were landing. He could feel the jar in wrists and arms. He was clubbed hard on the side of the head and knocked back against the wall. He came out and swung again, weaving, panting. A blow to the chest knocked him back. Once again he came out and then he found he was moving away from the wall. A kick landed high on his thigh. Then Tulsa fell against him, grabbed him around the waist, shoulder wedged under his chin. His rib cage creaked and bent. He was being bent backward at the waist. He felt behind himself. Tulsa had his left hand locked on his right wrist. He felt and found the broken hand and began to knead it, and felt the gritting of the broken bones. Tulsa inhaled sharply several times and then flung himself back.

Lloyd plodded after him and caught the left wrist in both his hands. Tulsa tried to twist free but he could not. He held the wrist and twisted it inward. Tulsa resisted. They stood there motionless. He felt the resistance slackening. Tulsa's whole body turned until Lloyd was behind him. He pulled the wrist higher until it was between Tulsa's wide shoulders, until the man began to bend forward from the waist. Then, with what was left of his strength, he pushed him forward, off balance, pushed hard, gained speed, ran him head-on into the concrete wall fifteen feet away. Tulsa fell and Lloyd fell on him. He pulled himself free. He crawled a few feet away and sat down with his back against the wall, head on his knees, hands resting slack on the floor, eyes closed, drawing agonizingly deep breaths into his lungs.

It took a long time for his breathing to slow. He got up slowly, and leaned one hand against the wall for support. He moved closer to Tulsa and looked down at him. Tulsa was utterly still. He bent over, grasped a massive upper-arm, and heaved him over onto his back. The eyes were half open. The big chest was still. The left side of the forehead, from temple to brow, was crushed flat.

Lloyd brought the laundry hamper over. He turned it back onto its side and worked the big body into it. He pulled it back up onto the wheels, and covered him with the soiled linen. He opened the door. He pushed the hamper into a far corner. He turned out the two lights. He walked through the sub basement until he came to a service elevator for the staff wing. He had good fortune. He reached his room without anyone seeing him, and the door was not locked. He washed and changed. There was a small contusion under his left eye, a long scratch over his right eye. It amazed him there could be so little visible damage. But his middle was so sore he moved like a very old man.

He packed his few belongings and carried the single suitcase down to the car. It was eleven thirty. He walked across the dark grounds and slipped into the heavy shrubbery by Danton's cottage. He could hear Latin American music. He moved cautiously to where he could look in one of the living room windows. Harry sat at the far end of the room. He was in his shirtsleeves. There was a briefcase on the floor beside him. He was reading typewritten pages.

The blonde girl was dancing by herself, in a dreamy graceless way. Her hips were heavy and she contributed a vulgar counterpoint of bump and grind. She wore red and white candy-striped slacks and a blue sweater. In her slow circuits of the room she would pause each time by the record player to take her drink from a shelf and take a single swallow.

He saw Harry speak angrily to her, but could not hear what he said. The girl went over and sat in a deep chair and sulked. He watched Harry and knew this would have to be an end of it, that it should be finished here at this time and in this place. The girl yawned and stretched, got up and wandered out the far door to the small pool. The pool lights were not on. He circled the building, silent, patient, cunning as an animal. He watched and could not see her. Finally he saw the flare of a lighter, and then the red glow of her cigarette. She was sitting in one of the aluminum chairs on the far side of the pool. There was starlight in the open. Avoiding the open places, he began to work his way around toward the girl. When he was quite close she snapped her cigarette into the pool. He waited, thinking she might get up and go in. He heard her sigh. He was close enough to see her tilt her head back and look up at the stars, blonde hair hanging down over the back of the chair. The records still played in the cottage.

He came up behind the chair. He could smell her perfume. He knelt behind her. He clapped one hand on her mouth, another around her waist, holding her in the chair.

She struggled convulsively, high heels clattering on the flagstones. He pulled her head back until she stopped struggling.

"If you make one sound," he said, "I'll kill you."

As he started to take his hand away, he heard the quick intake of breath which would give the scream more volume. He put his hand back, moved it until he could pinch her nostrils between thumb and finger. Soon she began to fight for breath. She scrabbled and tore at his hand with her nails. It took strength to hold her in the chair. Her efforts grew weaker and finally ceased. He held her for a few more seconds. When he released her, she slumped sideways over the arm. He lifted her out of the chair and laid her on the flagstones. He ripped open the waist of the slacks and pulled them off over her feet. The material tore easily. Her face was slack in the moonlight, mouth open. He leaned close. She breathed. He pushed half the sweater inside her mouth, tied it in place with a strip of material from the slacks. He tied her ankles, then rolled her over and fastened her wrists behind her. He pulled her into deeper shadows and rolled her under a bush.

He crouched for a time, listening. He stood up boldly and walked slowly to the cottage, walked through the open doors into the lighted interior. He stood half behind Harry's chair.

"Make me another drink, Selma," Harry said, not looking up. Lloyd did not move. Harry looked up in sudden irritation. Lloyd batted the papers out of his hand, snatched his wrists, yanked him out of the chair, swung him around and pushed him back into a corner away from the windows. He dropped one wrist, hit him hard. The glasses spun halfway across the room. As Harry sagged, Lloyd quickly felt of pockets and waist line. He then stepped back.

Harry shook his head, straightened himself up.

"Tulsa?" he asked.

"Dead, Harry."

Harry acceped that. "Now what?"

"What do you think?"

"I think I figured you wrong, kid. Right from the beginning. You turned out real hard. You come right in here and take both of them. That's a good trick."

"Let me know when you're through talking." He saw Harry glance beyond him, toward the glass doors. "Selma won't be coming in."

"We can make a deal, Wescott."

"No deal."

"You can come back. I'll cover you on Benny and Haynes and Selma. You can take over the hotel again. Run it your own way. I'll see you get a cut of the casino take. I'll give you a stock interest in the hotel corporation."

"No."

"Figure the angles. Do it your way and you're on the run. Do it my way and you'll live safe and live good. I can forget you crossed me. Hell, Benny and Tulsa did it. I wasn't even there."

"Your orders, Harry."

There was sweat on his forehead and Lloyd could smell the fear. "What good do I do you dead?" he asked. Lloyd knew he had tried to speak calmly, but the voice was pitched too high.

"What good does Sylvia do me?"

"Kid, she shilled you all the way. She was all tramp. Hell, she would have taken off with the dough first chance you gave her. She was a bum."

"Why did you marry a bum, Harry?"

"You got Benny and you got Tulsa."

"Yell, Harry. You built this place for privacy. Give a good yell and see who comes."

"I can understand you don't want to come back. How about this? I cover for the three of them and give you a hundred thousand in cash."

"No thanks. All I want is you, Harry."

"What good am I dead? What good does it do you?"

"I'm not going to kill you."

"Huh!"

"I'm not going to kill you, Harry. You know, you don't look like a hood. You look like a businessman. All I'm to do is give you a face like the one I'm wearing, Harry. You're going to look the part. I'm going to give you what you thought Tulsa was going to give me. You'll live, Harry. I found out I don't like to kill people. I'm not in your league. But I can give you a face you won't even know. Get set, Harry."

He put his hands up, palms outward. "Now wait a minute!"

"Get set, damn you!" He drew his right fist back, shoulder high.

Harry's hands fluttered. He made a curious sound. His eyes bulged and he stared at Lloyd, through Lloyd, stared off into some far place with an expression of enormous surprise. His mouth moved, but he said no words. He settled back against the wall and his knees bent slowly until he was crouched on his heels. His face was greyish. His head lowered and then snapped up so that it thumped against the wall, and the cords of his neck stood out. His eyes were turned up out of sight. His head sagged down until his chin was on his chest. Then he toppled over onto his side. His right hand scratched at the rug, his right leg twitched, and he lay still. Lloyd listened to his heart. He laid his ear on the chest and listened. There was a thready uncertain beat. As he listened it stopped. After a pause it beat four more times and stopped and would never beat again.

He stood up and wiped his hands on the sides of his trousers. He went to the bar and poured himself a stiff drink. In a little while he stopped trembling. He sat down and tried to think clearly. He decided what he would have to do if he wanted to gain time, but he could not bring himself to do it. Not for a long time.

At last he was able to close his mind, and work efficiently. He took the body into the bedroom. He closed the blinds, turned on the lights. He found silk pajamas under the pillow of one of the beds. He undressed Danton, got him into the pajamas, slid him into the bed, covered him over. He put the glasses on the night stand between the beds. He emptied the trouser pockets, hung the trousers in the closet. There was eight hundred and fifty dollars in the bill clip. He left one hundred and fifty.

Now the girl. He went out and picked her up, then

remembered that as yet she had not seen his face. He put her down, brought out a towel and made a tight blindfold. He could tell by the tensions of her body as he carried her in that she was conscious. He sat her on the edge of the other bed. She sat upright.

"You can hear me, Selma," he whispered. "Nod your head."

She nodded. She made a muffled sound behind the gag. Her nude body was white, suety and unpleasant to him. He went to the closet and brought back a pale blue satin robe. "I'm going to untie your hands. Don't reach for the blindfold. If you get a look at me, I'll have to kill you. Do you understand?" Again she nodded.

He reached around her and released her hands. She rubbed them together. He put the robe in her hands, then realized he had to help her put it on. Once she was in the robe and seated again he said, "Now I'm going to let you talk. Don't try to yell. There's nobody to hear you."

He pulled the gag from her mouth, dropped it on the floor. She made chewing motions and then licked her lips. "What the hell is going on? Who are you? Where's Harry?"

"Harry is dead."

"D'ya kill him?"

"He died of a heart attack or a brain hemorrhage or something."

She swallowed. "Where . . . is he?"

"Don't worry about where he is. I want you to answer some questions."

"Go to hell," she said weakly.

He slapped her, forehand and backhand. "You'll answer some questions."

"Okay."

"When do you usually get up?"

"Me, around noon."

"And Harry?"

"Earlier but not real early. Eleven maybe."

"Do you both ever sleep later?"

"After a rough night sometimes. Maybe two in the afternoon."

"Are there any sleeping pills around here?"

"In the bathroom cabinet. They're yellow. In a square bottle."

"How many does it take to knock you out?"

"I go out good on two."

"You're going to take four."

"What the hell for?"

"Here's what's going to happen. You're going to wake up very late. And you're going to find out that Harry died in his sleep. You're going to forget all about this, about my being here. Nobody would believe you anyway. Yell for the police, and you'll get involved."

"Is . . . is he in the other bed?"

"Yes. Right behind me. I'm sitting on the edge of it. He's in his pajamas."

"I dowanna sleep in here. Please, I dowanna."

"Don't try anything silly while I'm getting the pills, Selma. You can't get your ankles untied in time. If you pull that blindfold loose, you're going to take the whole bottle of pills. Then they can find both of you."

"I . . . I won't try anything. My God, that last record has played a thousand times."

He found the pills, held the bottle in a towel while he shook out four of them. He filled a tumbler with whisky and ice and took it to her, put it in her hand. He thought she might try to fake taking the sleeping pills. But the nearness of the body had cowed her. She took them meekly. Afterward she sipped steadily at the whisky. Her mouth became loose. Her words blurred. Twice she started to sag and fought to sit up again. The third time she toppled over. He let the whisky spill and the glass roll under the bed. He tried to awaken her and could not. He slipped the robe off and hung it up. He took off the blindfold and released her ankles, and put her into bed, covered her over. He turned out the room lights and opened the blinds. When he stood in the doorway he could hear her deep breathing.

When he turned off the record player the music died

sourly in the middle of a bar. He turned out the other lights, closed the glass doors, moved silently away into the night.

9

In all nations, in all the times of history, there have been wanderers, the men without goal or purpose, the self-ostracized. They have never been a group animal, a herd creature. There is no pattern to the wandering.

In the beginning Lloyd's wandering was flight. He had gained enough time so that he was able to withdraw his money from the bank of Oasis Springs. By nightfall he was five hundred miles from Oasis Springs, traveling northwest.

Had Charlie Bliss or one of his people found the body of Haynes, it is very probable that it would have been handled quietly, placed in some deep and unmarked grave out in sandy wastes. But the body was found by an old man who worked on the maintenance staff, a simple old man who despised the hotel, the guests, the gambling and all other employees. He looked with satisfaction at the body, covered it over again, put his broom away and went down to the town and made a report of murder to Carl Hand, the Chief of Police.

Even then it might have been handled in a different way, had Harry Danton been alive. Money can cause curious distortions of logic. With a few props, such as ladder and wrench, it might have been deduced that Haynes, while working on the overhead pipes, had fallen to his death, and perhaps bounced into the wheeled hamper. But Danton had died peacefully in his sleep, and Charlie Bliss did not have the executive talent to step in and secure official cooperation. As a matter of fact, the management of the Safari made it known to Hand that extreme diligence with the resultant bad publicity for the Hotel Green Oasis would not go entirely unrewarded. Had Danton been more generous with his partners, pressure might have been exerted from quite another direction.

But the deal at the Hotel Green Oasis had always been too fast and too tricky. And there were too many reputable and honest owners and managers of other hotels and casinos in the state—presuming, of course, that legalized gambling can ever be considered either reputable or honest—who saw in this incident a chance to make it nationally known that the gambling in the state is rigidly policed. State inspectors were happy to cooperate. Nobody of importance would be hurt. The various licenses were lifted—in fact, snatched. And it became illegal for the Hotel Green Oasis Corporation to conduct gambling, serve liquor, handle food or rent rooms. The career of Harry Danton, with emphasis on twenty-three arrests, five indictments, one conviction with suspended sentence appeared in both news and editorials. Herman "Tulsa" Haynes received almost equal coverage, though his batting average was much poorer. He had spent three and a half years in prison.

Due to his love for his fantasy comic books, Benny Bernholz had the secondary nickname of "Monster." This nickname appeared in the news items about him, without any explanation, permitting the reader to draw his own inference. The Monster was missing, and presumed dead. The publicity made a threatening motion in the direction of Charlie Bliss, but was quickly diverted by those who recognized Charlie's future value to other similar organizations. Old pictures of Sylvia appeared, along with cheesecake publicity poses of Selma, taken at the time she was doing an inept and lethargic strip on Burgundy Street. This was gang war, crookedness, lechery and murder, and must be stamped out. The big broom swept energetically. The Hotel Green Oasis was an echoing emptiness. Virtue had triumphed.

No sooner was it empty than the cautious negotiations began. This was a prize to be purchased cheaply. With a new name, a new corporation, new influence, it could one day be reopened, and would be reopened. It was unthinkable that it should not be used again.

Even the most lard-headed village cop would have begun to look for Robert Rose. He had left the hotel without notice. He had drawn a startlingly large amount of cash out of a checking account. They picked up three fair prints and one partial thumb print from his room. An artist made a sketch of him that seemed to satisfy the people who had worked with him. The sketch was enough to give tiny children the horrors. The make of car and license number was known. In view of the head start he had managed, a ten-state alarm went out.

He knew they were after him. He felt almost indifferent to the chase. Flight was automatic. Had he been frightened, he might have made mistakes. Being indifferent, he reacted with guile and intelligence. The beard was the most distinguishing characteristic. He shaved that off in cold water under a small California bridge. He abandoned the car by driving it into a large used car lot, removing the plates, folding them twice into a small packet and dropping them into a trash can a block away. That night, in a Los Angeles hotel, he used peroxide sparingly on his hair and brows until they grey blended with the lighter color, until the white patch was less obvious. He studied his face in the mirror. The naked face looked battered and savage, with a telltale pallor where the beard had been.

From there he moved north, making short trips by bus and train. He had destroyed all identification as Robert Rose. During that time he was nameless. When he arrived in Portland on a weekday morning, he looked up the address of the Wescott Lumber Company in the phone book, and took a taxi. When he went in he saw Tom standing in a doorway in his shirt sleeves, arguing with a man in work clothes. Lloyd waited until his brother turned to go back into his office and then said, "Tom."

Tom was older and heavier and not as tall. He stared at Lloyd. "Do I know you?"

Lloyd walked up to him. "You used to know me pretty well."

Tom stared. His face changed. "Lloyd," he whispered. "For God's sake. What . . . Come in."

He closed the office door. They shook hands. "We all decided you were dead. My God, I even paid a detective agency and they got noplace. What happened to you?"

"I was in a bad accident. Amnesia."

"Wasn't there any identification on you?"

"Apparently not."

"Have you tried to get in touch with mother?"

"I came here first."

"Dad died last year. She's living with us now. She's always talking about you, wondering what happened to you. She was the only one who wouldn't believe you were dead. This will . . . mean a lot to her."

And it meant a lot to her. He lived with them for three weeks. The house was not large enough for four adults and four children. He knew that Marge, Tom's wife, resented his presence. He knew he was not a good guest. There was no lightness in him. He could not make conversation. The children seemed wary of him. When Tom and his mother asked questions, he answered vaguely. There was both a restlessness and an emptiness in him. He could not feel close to these people. Tom and his mother loved a man who no longer existed. He sensed that Tom resented having the entire burden of the support of their mother.

He left without saying goodby. He left a note for Tom, and a note for his mother. With the note for Tom he left a shoe box containing twenty-five thousand dollars. He wrote, "In order to avoid questions, you probably should keep this in a safe place and feed it in as you need it. Don't worry about the source of it. I have no idea of where I will go or what I will do. Perhaps I should not have come back. Sometimes life reaches a dead end before you realize it or expect it."

And so another man joined the thin ranks of the wanderers.

Many knew him in far places, and wondered about him. When a man has gone beyond the point where he can feel fear or hope, there is a quality about him that sets him apart from others. There is an ominousness in his silences, and a hint of savage violence kept under careful control. The non-conformist is always suspect. Men saw the capacity for violence. Women saw lostness in the eyes, imagined a softness that hid behind the shattered face with its marks of mending.

A tall man with a ruined face worked in the Salinas Valley crops until he was brown as any Mexican.

A tall man worked the night trick at a fleabag hotel in Chicago, and left when the manager became too curious about his background.

For five months he helped a lonely woman run a North Carolina motel, sharing her drudgery, sharing her bed—and left one day without warning, leaving half the money he had saved in an envelope for her. She looked down the road in the direction he had gone, and knew she would never forget him or stop wondering about him.

As a vagrant in Georgia, a man who spoke in a manner that betrayed an education in contrast with a work-hardened body and a broken face, worked thirty days on the road.

He swung west, through the south, taking work that punished his body. But exhaustion could not blunt memory. And finally one day he knew where he was going and knew what would become of him, knew the meagerness of his own destiny.

A tall norteamericano walked through the mountain villages. His clothing was ragged and he carried a pack of great heaviness, the shoulder straps stained with his sweat. He had a great russet beard, and he spoke in the dialect of the mountain people of Queretaro. He was not like the turistas. He knew of the small customs and courtesies, and in return for food and a place to sleep, he would do the work of two. This was a strange one, with a manner of sadness. He followed the mountain trails rather than the highways.

At last, on a clear cold April day, after following the half-remembered trail past the places where steepness made the breath shallow and the heart fast, he rounded the rock shoulder and saw the huts and the steep slant of the fields, and women washing clothing in the stream below the waterfall. They were far below him, and tiny as small brown dolls.

Though he was weary, he quickened his pace. He reached the settlement. They gathered around him. He towered over them, smiling, walking slowly among them to the hut, to his own place. One of the women struck the iron bar that called the men back from the field.

Isabella was unchanged, and yet seemed a stranger to him. The child was three, a daughter named Carmencita, very shy of the tall stranger. And Isabella, too, was shy. There was news. There were four new huts. Now the settlement numbered thirty-five, soon to be thirty-six when Concha bore the child of Armando. Accompanied by Roberto, Rosario and Armando, he had to make a tour of the settlement to inspect the gifts he had sent which had so enriched them, had made life in this hidden and primitive place so much more endurable. The most appreciated gift was the box containing the school supplies, the many books and writing materials. Now there was a school, and the children would not grow up in ignorance.

They had a tact and understanding which not only prevented them from showing surprise at his return, but from either commenting on the surgery that had repaired his face, or the length of his absence. He knew they would ask no questions of him.

Isabella was more shy of him than she had been as a bride. The greatest liberty she permitted herself was to touch his face lightly with her fingertips, the tip of his nose, the reconstructed cheek, the diminished scar and say, "It is like a miracle." And then turn abruptly away.

They ate. He went with Roberto, Rosario and Armando to the flat rock, with a bottle of the mescal, and they sat where they could watch the blue dusk shadows fill the valley.

Roberto talked extravagantly of the great adventures of the twenty-three packing cases, of the electric excitement in the settlement as each was opened and the miracles displayed. He said, "With such luxuries, and with a school, it became necessary for this place to have a name, so that it may be thought of as a village instead of a hiding place. Much thought was given to the name, and of many choices, it was voted, we name it Nuevo Pinal Blanco. And, in the voting, Armando became mayor."

"A good choice," Lloyd said.

There was silence. The bottle was passed around. Roberto cleared his throat and said, "How long will you stay with us?"

"Toda mi vida," Lloyd said. All my life. "If it is permitted."

"We are pleased and honored," Armando said. "We are honored that you choose this small place over the comforts and excitements of your own land."

"My wife and my child are here. I went back and did what had to be done. One had died. Now the other three are dead."

"That is good," Rosario said.

"For a time I did not think to return here. But then it became necessary to me. It is satisfying to me to work with my hands. It is satisfying to me to sit here in this manner and drink from this bottle and talk with friends."

When he walked back through the night to his home, Isabella was waiting for him. She unrolled the pallets and fixed the bedding. He lay beside her in the darkness, not touching her. He told himself that he had retreated from life, that life had defeated him.

Yet he knew he had been drawn back here. Perhaps these mountains had marked his soul as deeply as they had marked his face. Armando had talked of the comforts and excitements. Spurious excitements of television and cinema. Dubious comforts of spoiled women.

For a long time he had kept something locked deeply inside him. He lay beside Isabella and he felt something inside him struggling to be free. It broke free, and there was a warmth in him, a warmth that filtered up and became tears to sting his eyes and thicken his throat.

He turned abruptly to her and gathered her roughly into his arms, and he could not control the hoarse sounds he made, the frightening sounds of the sobbing of a grown man.

She held him and soothed him and after a time he became aware of what she was saying to him, and when he heard her words he knew the depth of her understanding, and sensed how rewarding their life would be.

"It is all over now," she kept saying. "You have come home. It is all over now."

Of all the far places of the world, this was home.

69-10-2